I SEEK THE MIRACULOUS

BARBARA CARTLAND

SHELDON PRESS
LONDON

First published in Great Britain in 1978 by Sheldon Press,
Marylebone Road, London NW1 4DU

Printed in Great Britain by
Richard Clay (The Chaucer Press) Ltd
Bungay, Suffolk

ISBN 0 85969 135 7

The Author

Barbara Cartland, the celebrated romantic novelist, historian, playwright, lecturer, political speaker and television personality, has now written over two hundred books. She has had a number of historical books published and several biographical ones, including a biography of her brother, Major Ronald Cartland, who was the first Member of Parliament to be killed in the Second World War. The book has a preface by Sir Winston Churchill.

In private life, Barbara Cartland is a Dame of Grace of St. John of Jerusalem, and one of the first women, after a thousand years, to be admitted to the Chapter General.

She has fought for better conditions and salaries for midwives and nurses, and, as President of the Hertfordshire Branch of the Royal College of Midwives, she has been invested with the first Badge of Office ever given in Great Britain, which was subscribed to by the midwives themselves.

Barbara Cartland has also championed the cause of old people and founded the first Romany Gypsy Camp in the world. It was christened 'Barbaraville' by the gypsies.

Barbara Cartland is deeply interested in Vitamin Therapy and is President of the National Association for Health.

I Seek the Miraculous

This book is not an autobiography. I have written four describing my varied and exciting life, my crusades against injustice, my battles for Natural Health, and the famous and interesting people I have met over the years.

But I have also sought to discover the secrets which lie beneath the gaiety and the glory, the laughter and the tears.

I have now set down little incidents, insignificant perhaps in themselves, when I have been inspired, when I have had a glimpse of the World behind the World, and the times when I believed I stepped through the Looking Glass.

Also the times when I was disappointed and disillusioned.

It has been a thrilling and absorbing search and I hope that my experiences will perhaps help someone else a little towards the development of what the Greeks called the knowledge that 'I am I'.

BARBARA CARTLAND
May 1977

1907

Amerie Court
Pershore
Worcestershire

I am walking along a country road holding onto the perambulator which my Nanny is pushing. Inside it is my new baby brother Ronald who was born in January. I am very bored with having him with us and have already said to my mother:

"Mummy do let us send that baby away. Everyone asks after him and no-one asks after me!"

I think the real reason I resent him is that my mother looks at him in a different way from how she looks at me. Her eyes seem to have a light behind them and her voice is full of love.

I know now I am not part of her as I was before, but complete in myself, and I feel alone. Even when people are all round me I am alone and it's a strange and rather frightening feeling.

We reach a cottage where Nanny is to leave some soup for a woman who is ill. While she talks at the door I cross the road.

There is a gate into the park which is open. I stand beside it and look at the crimson poppies among the grasses, the purple cuckoo-flowers, the white and gold marguerites, and the blue love-in-the-mist.

Suddenly as I'm looking at them the flowers seem to come nearer to me, to get larger ... and larger.

There is a strange vibration coming from them and I think that I can see them growing ... living ... breathing ...

It is so extraordinary and so exciting that I stand

1

staring at the flowers and I know they are alive as I am.

"Barbara!" It is my Nanny's voice. "What are you doing? Come here at once, you naughty little girl!"

The spell is broken, I run back across the road . . .

1910

Pershore
Worcestershire

I know there are goblins with huge heads and little bodies burrowing beneath the hills. There are nymphs soft as the mist in the silver lakes and streams; huge green dragons, fighting and breathing fire, lurk in the darkness of the pine woods.

There are two big trees very close together in the secret part of the garden, and when I am going to sleep I know that if I can squeeze between them I shall find all that I am seeking, although I am not certain what it is.

Sometimes I have a glimpse of a fairy amongst the flowers – I see her out of the corner of my eye, but when I turn my head she has gone.

The fairies dance on the lawn at night and leave a circle of mushrooms; so I know they have been there.

In the winter when the leafless branches of the trees are silhouetted against the sunset I have a strange feeling within me as if they lift me up into the sky.

1912

Pershore
Worcestershire

I have read *Alice Through the Looking-Glass* and I know now that what I have been trying to do before I go to sleep is to step through the Looking-Glass.

That is the world that fascinates and draws me, the world I sense between the trees, the world of the Goblins and Fairies, a world behind the world.

I know it is very near me, a shadow behind my head, just round the corner, at the top of the stairs.

I am determined to find it.

Sometimes when I am alone in the garden I put my ear against the trunk of a tree. I can hear it breathing and living. Everything has life in it like the life in me.

But there is another part of life which I cannot hear or touch, yet it is there through the Looking-Glass.

1914

❦

Bath
Somerset

I have seen an angel! I am unhappy in the house where I am staying and the girl with whom I am doing lessons is unkind to me.

I was in my bedroom thinking of my mother and praying, when on the wall in front of me I saw the huge outline of an angel. His head nearly touched the ceiling and his feet were only a few inches off the floor.

He was outlined in light like a drawing and only his wings had any substance. He did not move and his face which was very beautiful was turned sideways.

I knelt looking at him in amazement for perhaps sixty seconds, then slowly he faded.

Addition: It was not until many years later that I realised my angel was like a drawing by Michelangelo; the same magnificent lines, the same noble head as is depicted in the Sistine Chapel in Rome.

1916

Nailsea Court
Somerset

I am living in a ghost house. There is always someone going up the stairs ahead of me or coming up behind; yet they can't be seen.

The house is very old and filled with the panelling and furniture of Judge Jeffreys – the Hanging Judge. Has his bitterness and cruelty still survived?

I am never alone. Last night I heard footsteps dragging their way upstairs, and the tick of the clock like the beat of a heart sounded loudly in my ears.

I was terrified and could only pray desperately:

"Lighten our darkness, we beseech Thee, O Lord and by Thy great mercy defend us from all perils and dangers of the night . . ."

The footsteps stopped at my door.

To-day I have learnt that a Cavalier who had been wounded by the Roundheads came back here to die.

Addition: Years later when I think of this house I wrote this poem:

"TO A GHOST"

I heard your footsteps coming up the stairs,
Or were you moving just ahead?
I keep on wondering who you are and where
You lie unknown.

I hear you move across the room and sigh,
I hear you close the door and wonder why.
What do you regret? I half suspect
You hate to be alone.

Whisper your secret, let me share your crime,
Or are you seeking someone all the time
You love, and whom you cannot find,
In body, soul or mind?

Can empty arms, an aching heart,
Survive the grave, and must we part
With flesh, to suffer still more pain
'Til we return and live again?

1916

Nailsea Court
Somerset

Living in the Ghost House in quiet countryside I hear very little about the war and the mud, blood and horror of the trenches.

A jolly, middle-aged Major comes to stay and he is obviously pleased with my wide-eyed interest in him. He offers to show me his service revolver and brings it into the billiard room where we are alone. He demonstrates how a soldier releases the chamber which contains five bullets.

"Now it's empty," he says.

Jokingly he points it at me and pulls the trigger. He has forgotten the sixth bullet in the chamber! It whizzes through my hair at the side of my head and with a deafening report buries itself in the wall behind me!

I have never before seen a man go deadly pale.

"Don't tell anyone," he begs.

I haven't and he tips the Estate carpenter to plaster up the damaged wall.

I am deaf in one ear and I wonder what it would have been like to be dead.

1917

Nailsea Court
Somerset

I have been confirmed and every Sunday I bicycle about a mile and a half to early Communion in a very old Church.

Beside it stands a beautiful Manor house built in the time of Charles I, but now it is deserted, its windows boarded up, the door locked.

Sometimes for fun we go over with friends and try to get in, but never succeed.

The local story is that the family who lived in it for generations and who were Roman Catholics began to be haunted by an evil monk.

He made their lives so intolerable that they asked a Cardinal to exorcise him.

The Cardinal performed the Service of Exorcism and said he would sleep in the ghost room.

He was asleep when he awoke with a start to see the monk standing beside his bed. Before he could pray or even make the Sign of the Cross the monk struck him and rendered him unconscious.

He was ill for a long time and when he recovered he said the family must leave the house with its evil influences to fall to the ground.

The Church is even older than the house. It has sunk through the centuries or the ground has risen around it, and now one walks down several steps to the aisle.

There is a smell of age and dust and it is very dark because the stained glass windows are old and dirty and the two candles on the altar cast an inadequate light.

There are present only the Parson who takes the

service, a server, and two very old women besides myself.

As I kneel in an ancient pew, I know that there are many more people in the Church than can be seen.

I can feel them behind me, I can even hear them breathing, and if they are dead they are still tied to the earth.

It is strange, eerie yet fascinating, and although there are other Churches I could attend, I go back Sunday after Sunday to the one where those who lived in the haunted house worshipped for centuries.

1918

Tewkesbury
Worcestershire

My mother was staying with her mother. She had been to Cheltenham with my younger brother, Tony, to see a doctor who said he must have his tonsils out at once.

As soon as she reached home the butler came into the room with a telegram. Even as my mother took it she knew what she would read.

War Office.
Deeply regret Major J. B. F. Cartland Worcester Regt. killed in action May twenty seventh. Army Council express sympathy.

Secretary War Office

My mother was prostrate, she had been so happy in her married life and together she and my father had survived and surmounted so many difficulties

She arranged a Memorial Service to take place in Tewkesbury Abbey on June 17th. That very morning, as she was dressing to go to early Communion at which special prayers were to be said for my father, she received another telegram from the War Office:

Major J. B. F. Cartland Worcester Regiment previously reported killed in action now reported missing May 27th and not killed further news when received.

My mother was too overjoyed and excited for words. The Memorial service was put off, telegrams being sent in every direction; mourning clothes were laid aside.

Then began a terrible time of waiting and of slowly

dying hope. Every time that my mother left the house she hurried the last hundred yards on her return and her first glance was for the hall table where the telegrams were laid.

She had interviews at the War Office, the Red Cross Prisoners of War Organisation, and visited wounded soldiers in hospitals.

Fortune-tellers and clairvoyants had sprung up in their thousands during the war when anxiety drove wives and mothers to any course, however desperate, which might bring comfort and keep hope alive.

My mother had a letter from a great friend, who had been her bridesmaid and who had married soon after she did, to say she was sure my father was alive.

Her husband had been killed early in the war after some years of great happiness and she had 'got in touch' with him through a Medium and 'spoke to him' regularly every week. At her last séance her husband had 'come through' to say that my father was alive, but in a German hospital.

My mother was only too anxious to clutch at any straw, however slender, and her friend wrote again and again, always with encouraging reports that my father was alive. But there was no official news all through July.

In August my mother took us all to Budleigh Salterton in Devonshire for a holiday. We all went to a Garden Fête there in aid of the Red Cross. There was a fortune-teller and my mother went into a little tent to have her hand read for 2s. 6d.

Dressed as a gipsy, the woman looked at my mother's palm and said conversationally:

"I see you are a widow . . ."

My mother burst into tears but managed to pull herself together and watch Tony run in a race and the others win prizes at the hoop-la. When she got home, she wept all night.

On September 23rd my mother had a letter from the War Office saying that it was now known that my father had been killed in the trenches with his men. But the shells and trench mortar bombs raining on the British trenches had left the ground as though it had been ploughed – there were few identifiable bodies and no personal belongings which could be returned to the relatives.

1918

London

The war is over and the four long years have seemed interminable.

I had watched my mother go pale and fight for self-control at the sight of a telegraph boy coming to the door.

I had watched her open a yellow envelope with trembling fingers, and though there had often been a glad cry of:

"How wonderful! Daddy's coming home on leave!" there was eventually that inevitable moment when she read the telegram which began: "The Secretary of State for War regrets . . ."

But that was not all. In thousands and thousands of homes like my own the male member of the family on active service is "missing".

This was perhaps the worst of all to endure. My father was actually presumed dead, reported missing, and now again presumed dead.

We who are growing up will never forget those long-drawn-out days when we waited for the postman, when letters came from friends or comrades of my father saying they thought he was a prisoner. We shall never forget the speculation which went on and on day after day, week after week, month after month, as we wondered where he might be, what he was doing, whether he was wounded, whether he was being well treated.

Every story we heard of the way the Germans treated their prisoners was another twist of the knife in the wound.

I lived through it all, every moment, every anxiety,

every horror of it, until the final memorial service with its rendering of the Last Post.

Of course it left its mark upon me; four years is a very long time in the life of a child or an adolescent.

Now the war is over I am sick of it all. I can't go on living under the dark strain with those tears and miseries; I can't bear all those anniversaries:

"The anniversary of the day that Daddy was reported missing."

"The anniversary of the day that he was reported killed."

"The anniversary of the day he last came home on leave."

"His birthday."

I am trying to become detached from it all and to dance and dance and dance.

1920

London

The widows and the families of those who have been killed in the war long to get in touch with those they loved. There are séances in many people's houses.

I have just been to one which made me angry because I think those who performed were trying to 'coin-in' on the unhappiness of those who are bereaved.

There was present a mixture of young and old. The first Medium, we were told, was the incarnation of an Egyptian princess – they are always Royalty, I notice. When I arrive she is demanding brandy.

"I can't loosen up without it."

When she had drunk a good deal she danced, dressed in a chiffon scarf wrapped round her breasts and folded between her legs.

"She must be controlled by an Egyptian!"

"Wonderful! Like a frieze in Luxor!"

"I can feel the spirits round her!"

Personally I thought it a pathetic performance brought on by alcohol.

After this another Medium managed with many contortions to apport from her back a bunch of pink roses.

I was told she had been examined by two ladies before the séance, but I doubted if it was very thorough.

"The flowers have the dew of Paradise on them," someone in the audience exclaimed hysterically.

I thought it was water out of the tap, but when I said something of the sort to my hostess she was horrified.

"You must not upset anyone!" she exclaimed. "They believe in the Medium."

It was all very pathetic, the blind desire to be convinced. So I was silent.

A story which I find very impressive concerns the mother of Lord Glenconner with whom I often dance.

Lady Glenconner has lost another and dearly loved son in the war and she took her own photographic plates to a Spirit Photographer.

He is an ordinary working-man who, she was told, had produced portraits of those who had 'passed on'.

Lady Glenconner's close friends were afraid of fraud, which would have been quite easy as photographs of the young man had appeared in all the illustrated papers at the time of his death.

A portrait, I am told, has appeared on the plates but it is not of Lady Glenconner's son.

Instead it is of an unimportant man to whom she had once been engaged and who had loved her deeply until his death a year ago.

17

1920

London

There is still an enormous overlap from the previous generation. One doesn't suddenly become different – the change is very gradual, sometimes almost imperceptible.

So Edwardian London is still all around us, and we are living with Edwardian people. We have not yet any history or identity of our own.

London in 1920 is structurally unchanged from the Edwardian days. Gas-light is still common in the private houses.

Piccadilly is lined by dignified mansions and clubs; the great houses, such as Devonshire, Grosvenor, Dorchester, Lansdowne and Londonderry are all inhabited by their owners.

Devonshire House has magnificent wrought-iron gates tipped in gold facing into Piccadilly.

It was from this house that the blonde, lovely Georgina, Duchess of Devonshire, a compulsive gambler, emerged to canvass for Charles James Fox in the Westminster Election of 1784, and bought a vote from a butcher with a kiss.

It was here, after her death, that her greatest friend Lady Elizabeth Foster – dearest Bess – having secretly given birth to two children married the Duke.

In my mother's day the Devonshires were spoken of with awe and respect, despite the fact that the Duke was nicknamed 'Harty Tarty' and the Duchess 'Grand Slam'.

She wore a yellow-red wig and was obsessed by the new deviation of whist which was called bridge.

I am interested in people who are dead or too old for me to meet them, but it seems to me that the gates of Devonshire House and the great high walls have a special magical quality for stimulating the imagination.

Behind its garden there is Lansdowne House – of perfect Adam design – facing into Berkeley Square, and separating these two princely mansions is a narrow passage, which is a private right of way.

One day every year Lord Lansdowne sends men to lock and bolt the doors at each end of the passage, but for the other 364 days it is available as a short cut between Curzon Street and Berkeley Street.

Many crimes have taken place in Lansdowne Passage, with its high, sightless walls; but it is not the stabbings, the robberies, or the vile assignations that I think about when I walk through Lansdowne Passage, or the beautiful, passionate Devonshires, but of the ghost which is reputed to haunt it.

1920

London

I am engaged and it has been formally announced in the Court column of *The Times*.

Terence Langrishe is the only surviving son of Sir Hercules Langrishe, a delightful Irishman who has a thirteenth-century castle in Ireland.

'Pingo', as my fiancé was nicknamed, served in France in the Irish Guards; he has a keen sense of humour, is charming, impetuous and practically penniless.

My mother has insisted that he must get a job before we get married. She might just as easily have asked him to kill the proverbial dragon of the fairy stories.

Employment is something every one is seeking. There are actually 353,000 unemployed ex-soldiers.

London is filled with men with magnificent war records and empty pockets; I have seen them in queues outside factories hoping to be taken on; I find them wandering into fashionable restaurants just before luncheon hoping to meet someone who will offer them a meal.

Every business man I am told had a pile of letters of personal recommendation and applications, hoping for a vacancy. In the country, chicken farms, wayside garages and tea-houses have sprung up like mushrooms, all run by ex-service men.

Many of these have already gone bankrupt and their owners have joined the patient queues of hollow-eyed men who, by a nervous movement, a twitching muscle or a too rigid tension, betray that they are all in some greater or lesser degree suffering from shell-shock.

Men are not at all particular as to what they do. My grandmother has employed as a temporary butler a Colonel with a D.S.O. When my partner hails a taxi on leaving a restaurant or a dance he will often look at the driver and ejaculate: "Hello, old boy!" or even occasionally: "How are you, Sir?"

The Government expecting a peace boom, gave a free unemployment insurance policy to every member of the fighting forces below commissioned rank, but nothing was done for the ex-officer. Traditionally a gentleman, he is supposed to have private means.

Finding no work in England, Pingo joined a Secret Police Force which has been sent to Ireland. But this means he will be away for at least six months.

The relations between Ireland and England through the nineteenth century have been a story of one long, tragic misunderstanding. Before the war Mr. Asquith introduced Home Rule which became law in 1914.

Ulster refused to be included in the new State and the Great War averted Civil war. In 1916 a rebellion broke out in Dublin which, savagely suppressed, gave birth to a fierce, burning nationalism.

The Sinn Fein Republican Government came into active opposition to the British administration, and a special police force, known as the "Black and Tans", showed great savagery, because to them the Irish rebels were traitors.

Now there is to be a small supplementary force of picked men from England as a Special Police Force.

Pingo left for Dublin and with him also in search of a job has gone a great friend Peter Ames, a particularly delightful person, one of the 'tall Ames' and a member of the Brigade of Guards.

He had recently become engaged to my best friend Millicent Orr Ewing. Her father had been killed in the South African War.

Pingo and Peter arrived in Ireland in September.

I get a letter every day from my fiancé. They are very loving, but they give me an inexplicable feeling of tension, of waiting for something catastrophic to happen.

Pingo treats everything which is happening as a joke, but I feel as if I am back in the war, feeling sick at the sight of a telegram ... waiting ... waiting ...

The telegram arrives. It is almost as if everything has happened before and is just being repeated.

"Peter killed this morning. Tell Millicent. Love Pingo."

On November 21st – "Bloody Sunday" – ten officers and four other ranks serving in the Special Police Force were murdered in their beds.

Case 38. Upper Mount Street. Two murders. House entered 9.10. a.m. 20 armed, unmasked men let in by servant, Catherine Farrell, who unwillingly pointed out rooms occupied by Lt. Ames of the Grenadier Guards and Lt. Bennett of the R.A.S.C. Motor Transport. Maid rushes upstairs and told officer sleeping on upper floor and another male lodger that murder was being done downstairs. Fusillade shots heard. When they came downstairs they found two bodies in a pool of blood in Ames's bedroom. Bennett evidently dragged from bed in bed clothes into brother officer's room where both shot together, their bodies lying side by side.

I took a bus to Hill Street and went to tell Millicent.

I can still see the railings of the houses as I walked slowly down the street, up the steep stairs of her house which led to her own little sitting-room on the top landing – a room where she had planned her future with Peter ...

Yesterday on December 7th a Requiem Mass was sung for Peter Ames in Westminster Cathedral. Soldiers with inverted arms guarded his unusually long coffin which lay in state under a Union Jack.

Sitting in the Cathedral I felt a sudden horror of Ireland, of violence and perhaps unreasonably of all Irishmen!

I shall break off my engagement.

1921

Nailsea Court
Somerset

I am at Nailsea Court where I stayed during the war. A young Irishman is also here. He says he is psychic and can read people's reincarnations in previous lives.

He tells me that in one life I was Roman, the daughter of an important member of the Senate. I am betrothed to a Patrician but have a love affair with the gladiator who is teaching my young brother to fight.

Nero finds out about my intrigue and orders a fight between the man I am to marry and the gladiator.

The gladiator wins and holds the Patrician with a sword at his throat. He looks to Nero for the sign to kill or show mercy.

Nero turns to me and says it is my decision, but if it is one of mercy, the gladiator must kill himself.

It all sounds an amusing fantasy but for some time I have had a recurring dream in which I am being carried on a litter up a long flight of steps.

I see nothing more than my outstretched feet, the curtain which covers the top of the litter and the steps.

The Irishman also says that in the large Dining-Room which has walls covered with ancient oak panelling and diamond paned windows there is a young woman.

She is weeping bitterly and pleading for her life. She has long fair hair falling over her shoulders.

He tells the tale so vividly that I never go into the Dining-Room without thinking I can see her and hear her piteous cries.

Addition: Many years later some alterations have to be
made to the chimney-piece, and in moving the hearth-
stone the workmen find the skeleton of a young woman.
As she is uncovered they see she has long fair hair, which
in the passing of a second crumbles into dust.

1921

London

I am in love and he has a car! Nothing could be more exciting than to be conveyed away into the night beyond restrictions, chaperons and convention. It is an unbelievable enchantment.

I have written down what it means to me.

"ENCHANTMENT"

Your headlamps like two golden moons
Shine on the silver way,
The wind is singing you faery tunes;
Drive on till you find the day.
Adventures are there in the dusky trees
There where the blue mists lie,
Adventures crooned by the murmuring breeze
To the flowers – their lullaby.
Have you forgotten Peter Pan,
Tink and the pirate crew,
The song of the jungle Mowgli sang,
The cry the wolf-pack knew?
Down in the cities the flaring lights
Of brothel, bar and street
Are filled with gaudy 'fly-by-nights',
Those vultures seeking meat.
Here, with the flickering lights away,
Away in the night-hid town,
You will, perhaps, hear an angel say:
'Why the stars have fallen down'.
Over the hills and far away
Your headlamps like golden moons
Driving on till the break of day,
With the wind-sung faery tunes.

25

1922

London

Last night I motored out of London after a dance. It was very exciting because I knew I really ought not to be alone with a young man in the country after dark.

We drove towards Kingston and turned off the road up a small track which led to a wood of silver birch trees.

The moon was full and its beams, shining through the branches, were great shafts of light, blinding, beautiful, mysterious and compelling.

I felt I had only to walk into them and I . . . I would hear . . . I would understand . . . I would know . . . all the things I have tried to discover.

"You look strange," my partner said. "What's the matter?"

"I'm going to find out . . ." I answered incoherently.

"What do you mean?" he questioned. "What are you going to find out?"

"I'm not certain," I replied, "but it's something I've searched for all my life . . something I must . . learn."

He caught me by the shoulders and turned me round.

"Stop it!" he said. "You're far away from me and I don't like it."

He kissed me and drove me back to the main road, but I shall never forget how very nearly I found out the truth.

1922

London

I have discovered the Indian Love Lyrics and they awake something in me which I feel I have always known but have been unable to express.

> *We are ever and always the slaves of these,*
> *Of the suns that scorch and the winds that freeze.*

Why does that seem to echo in my mind? And

> *To love or not we are no more free*
> *Than a ripple to rise and leave the sea.*

I read the lyrics over and over again and long for something which is beyond thought and yet can be felt by a hidden sense.

> *For this is wisdom: to love and live,*
> *To ask what Fate or the Gods may give.*

I have written my own poem to try to express what I feel:

"*YEARNING*"

> *I want — I stretch out hungry hands*
> *To dreams which always evade my touch.*
> *And treasures of wisdom from ancient lands*
> *Are lost because I ask too much.*
>
> *Did I ever know the mystic truth*
> *Which sometimes a word will help recall?*
> *Bitterly in my soul's sweet youth*
> *I've learnt that idols fall.*

27

I want – the blue grey mountain mists,
The shadowy darkness of forest trees.
The rough waves by the moonbeams kissed
Hurt me – like falling leaves.

1923

Knocke Sur Mer
Belgium

My mother has taken my brothers and me to Knocke for the holidays.

To-day we hired a car and drove to Messines Ridge where my father had been in 1917. It has been a cold, bleak day with a promise of rain.

As we stood in the desolation of brown, churned earth, of countless shell-holes, of crumbling trenches, of charred tree stumps, of broken dug-outs, of rusty, tangled wire and rough wooden crosses, I realised for the first time a little of what war could mean.

A torn and tattered piece of sacking moved in the breeze across the doorway of a dug-out. The boys, excited and curious, pulled it aside. An officer's field boot was dislodged and it fell from the dug-out towards us.

Inside it were the skeleton bones of what had once been a leg.

Further on they picked up a tin hat which had a hole nearly drilled through the front just where a bullet would enter a man's forehead.

We drove on along the Menin Road where, in September 1917 a stream of troops amid a hail of artillery shells had trudged along duck board tracks into an inferno of fire and slaughter from which few returned.

In the distance we saw the gaunt grey devastation of what had once been the proud city of Ypres.

It was all very silent without a sign of life, everything barren and still like death.

It filled me with an indescribable horror I shall never be able to forget.

1923

❧

London

I am very superstitious. When the Earl of Carnarvon died this year ostensibly of a mosquito bite, everyone knew it was due to "The Curse of the Pharoahs".

Lord Carnarvon and Howard Carter had discovered Tutankhamun's tomb, and when he died in Cairo there was a complete power failure of the electricity throughout the city, for which the technicians could find no technical explanation.

I was told that King Fuad of Egypt had said when the tomb was discovered:

"It is ill work. The dead must not be disturbed, only evil can come of it. Those who desecrate the resting-places of the ancient dead do so at their own peril. You will see."

Later I learn that a fox terrier bitch which Lord Carnarvon loved had at the exact moment of his death sat up in her basket, howled and fallen back dead.

1923

London

I have begun to see the tinsel beneath the gold. I long for something beyond the noise of nightclubs, the gossip, the chatter of little things, and yet I do not know where to find what I want.

The waves are breaking on the sand,
Above are golden stars,
The wind's a'blowing from the land,
Bearing the scent of flowers.
Alone? With all my secret dreams
Which nothing coarse or lewd
Can touch? Yet to the world it seems
That this is solitude.

Faces and a hundred tongues;
Money bred this dust.
Sensation welcomed when she comes
By drunken, brainless lust.

Somewhere a shrieking saxophone
Yells in its tonelessness
Of children, mother, love and home!
God! This is loneliness.

1923

London

I am beginning to look for an esoteric meaning in everything and wherever I go. But last night I had a moving and very emotional experience when I was taken to *Hassan*, a play by James Elroy Flecker, produced with music by Delius.

It is a blend of beauty, poetry, music, colour, drama and tragedy.

It is the story of a man with poetry in his soul – a confectioner in Arabia who fell in love and sought his ideal only to find he had lost all he had . . . and then he started all over again.

Watching I felt I was a pilgrim – reciting Flecker's wonderful words:

> *We are the pilgrims, master; we shall go*
> *Always a little further: it may be*
> *Beyond that last blue mountain barred with snow,*
> *Across that angry or that glimmering sea.*

Hassan remains in my mind. It is not only its beauty I remember so vividly, but it has given me an uncontrollable urge to explore the world. The East draws me.

I keep repeating some lines from the play. They are music. They are what I hear when I listen to the wind in the trees.

Flecker died in 1915, another life lost, and yet he has left so much behind.

1925

London

I have never believed in fortune-tellers except one – Mrs. Robinson, whom everyone visits in her tiny flat up flights of stone steps near Olympia.

When she read Winston Churchill's hand in 1898 she 'saw' such an exciting and brilliant future ahead of him that, while praising her 'strange skill in palmistry', he asked her not to publish it.

Her prophetic picture of him was –

"Of a man holding back a pair of iron gates against a mob of millions with arms outstretched."

Among Mrs. Robinson's clients were Lily Langtry, who took Edward VII to visit her, Oscar Wilde, Lord Roberts, and Shane Leslie.

She tells me the initials of the man I shall marry, when in fact I am in love with someone quite different; so it was certainly not thought-reading!

1926

Worcestershire

This evening I was motoring in the dark along a country road with a man who is a very good driver. Suddenly I screamed:

"Stop! Look out!" and put my hand over my eyes.

He asks me quite calmly what is wrong and I reply that I saw him quite clearly driving into a flock of sheep.

A little further on we stop for dinner at a hotel and learn that three years ago a car did drive into a flock of sheep at that very spot!

Ghosts, in many cases, are photographs.

A violent crime is committed, the vibrations of murderer and victim are so strong that they charge the atmosphere with a permanent photograph of what has occurred.

Sometimes certain weather conditions are required to develop the negative clearly for ordinary eye-sight, sometimes only mediumistic and clairvoyant people, whose sensibilities are peculiarly sympathetic, can perceive what has occurred.

But the photograph is there all the time and, so far as we know, for ever.

What people call evil spirits are often the result of a strong personality pouring out into the air vibrations of life from themselves.

A person with an intensely vital and strong character emits from himself strong vibrations directed with concentrated will-power.

Scientists have proved that our emotions, either good or bad, carry from ourselves atoms of life. When we concentrate on another person we pour towards them a feeling that is definitely *alive*.

When inanimate things are cursed, when a so-called evil spirit lurks in a room, it is because concentrated venom has accumulated there.

This force of evil is *alive* because what *is* of life cannot die.

I remember in Somerset several people told me that they had seen a coach drawn by four horses come tearing down a hill near Nailsea Court and crash at the bottom of it.

They told me they not only saw the accident, they heard it.

This is of course a photograph of what took place but the sound is more difficult to explain.

1926

London

Ronald and I have been experimenting with Time. A book called *An Experiment with Time* has been written by J. W. Dunne.

He proved quite simply that when we are asleep we are released from the imprisonment of this Dimension and see in our dreams images from the past, the present and the future.

"Look at it this way," Ronald reasons. "If we are leaving England in a ship for New York, to-day we are in Southampton, to-morrow in the open sea. New York is in the future. But if we were high enough up in the air and out of Time then we could see Southampton, the Atlantic and New York all as to-day and this moment."

I have written down my dreams the moment I awake and find innumerable times that I do dream of what had happened yesterday, and what was going to happen to-day and to-morrow.

1927

London

People often say: "I can't think why I am so depressed, just like a cloud pressing on me, while I have nothing to worry about".

It is not a bad description of what may actually have happened.

The waves along which our own personal vibrations travel and which emanate from ourselves are curved at the ends.

This is because being our own they can only stretch so far as our capabilities will allow them, and must return to us, even though the vibrations themselves can be released.

For instance, if we meet someone we do not like, we actually contract our personality waves, pulling them inwards while the contrary happens towards someone we like.

Then our vibrations pouring outwards embrace the vibrations of the other person, and we become 'friends'.

Some people force their vibrations upon others. In those cases one has the feeling that the person is too overpowering, and one has the instinct of withdrawal from them.

It is our own vibrations contracting.

1928

Orkney
The Shetland Isles

To-day I stood on the high cliffs in Orkney and looked below at the sea swirling round the rocks near where the *Hampshire* had been blown up by a German mine in 1916.

Everyone in her was drowned, including Field Marshal Lord Kitchener who was on a mission to Russia.

He had been an overwhelming personality of the war, and everywhere one looked there had been posters of him saying: "*Your King and Country need you.*"

I felt in that wild windswept spot I would sense something of the fear, the despair of those who had lost their lives.

Lord Kitchener's death was attributed, as Lord Carnarvon's had been, to the curse which lay on those who disturbed the resting-places of the dead.

Winston Churchill had criticised his action in permitting the sacred shrine of the Mahdi in the Sudan to be destroyed.

The curse proclaimed that – "he who desecrates the graves of religious leaders will perish through water floods and the place of his sepulchre will never be known".

I had heard that just before Lord Kitchener went aboard the *Hampshire* he told the famous astrologer Cheiro – who in private life was Count Hamon – that if anything happened to him he would give him a sign.

Cheiro was in the music room of his house abroad when a large hatchment (a coat of arms used when there was a death in the house) fell with a crash and split in two.

Cheiro guessed something had happened to Lord Kitchener and found out later it had fallen at the very hour the *Hampshire* went down.

Cheiro, I learn, had read Lord Kitchener's hand in 1894 and had told him:

"I can see nothing but success and honours for you in the next two decades. You will become one of the most illustrious men in the land.

"But after that your life is at great risk. I see a disaster at sea taking place in your sixty-sixth year."

1930

London

The twenties have come to an end. I am twenty-eight, married and no longer called "Flaming Youth" or a "Bright Young Person".

But I have learnt a lot, progressed a little in my inner search for my real-self and the world behind the world.

But to me looking back, the years after the war were wildly exciting and a period of inexpressible gaiety.

Like all my contemporaries I snatched at the wings of happiness and felt they lifted me towards the stars.

Like Peter Pan I cried:

> *I am youth, I am joy, I am the little*
> *bird which has broken out of the egg.*

I was young, I was alive, I could laugh and love and my feet could dance. That was ecstasy, that was youth, and it can never come again.

1930

The whole nation has been shocked by the Meopham Air disaster. The aeroplane fell to pieces in the air over Kent for no reason that can be discovered.

It is, everyone says, one of the great flying mysteries which will never be solved.

George Henderson, the pilot, was in love with me for a year. He was the famous flying ace and the first pilot to fly under Tower Bridge.

His face had been burnt in the war and he was somewhat disfigured. Because I was sorry for him I was nicer to him than I might have been otherwise, with the result that he fell in love with me.

He used to follow me wherever I went in his ugly, open, noisy car which was just an engine covered with iron plate and mounted on a chassis with two bucket seats taken from an aeroplane.

George called it "Barbed Arrow" a somewhat obscure play on my name. Because I christened it, he gave me a tiny diamond arrow, which was the latest craze in jewellery.

I tried to be fond of George but somehow, maybe because of his war experiences, he was one of those people who were touchy and difficult and always rubbed one up the wrong way.

He used to arrive wherever I was staying without warning in his enormous car, embarrassed, I had to manufacture explanations of his uninvited arrival.

As he was very jealous of any other man I knew, it created endless difficulties.

George had learnt to fly in 1915 and by the end of the war became a lieutenant-colonel in the Royal Flying Corps, which in those days used Army rank.

He flew for Daimler Airways and in 1924 joined the De Havilland Aircraft Company. Then he formed the Henderson School of Flying at Brooklands and started 'joy-riding' which operated at aviation meetings.

He opened several flying Schools in South Africa and inaugurated the passenger service from Cape Town to Johannesburg.

George had arrived at Croydon from Le Touquet in a large Junker monoplane and the machine was then over-hauled by engineers who declared it in perfect order.

But when he set off again, after eight minutes George returned saying he was worried by an unusual noise in the engine.

"A washer in the exhaust has begun to blow," the chief engineer explained. "Shall I replace it, sir?"

"Oh, no," George replied, "that's all right. So long as I know what it is, it doesn't matter."

He reached Le Touquet where he picked up the Marquess of Dufferin and Ava, Viscountess Ednam, Sir Edward Ward and Mrs. Henrik Loeffler, whose husband had owned the *Albion*, the largest steam yacht in the world, which he sold to Sir Thomas Lipton.

They reached Kent. Then in the pouring rain the aeroplane fell from the sky – the wreckage being strewn over an area of five miles.

There was no explosion, the petrol tanks were intact, the aeroplane was new, having only done 100 hours flying. All the vital parts of the engine were in order. The cylinder was uncracked.

No one will ever really know why the accident happened, but it has been suggested that power from another planet was involved – perhaps an electronic ray from a Flying Saucer?

1930

London

I am extremely interested in a curse which has been laid on an English Peer whom I know.

A big blustery noisy man, he was visiting North Africa with some friends. Robert Hichens, the author, showed them the sights, one of them being an ancient mosque.

As usual the doorkeeper asked them respectfully to remove their shoes, but the English Peer strode past him.

Inside the mosque, where the faithful were at prayer, a priest with a long beard and the high black hat of Islam stopped the Englishman and spoke to him in Arabic.

"I can't understand a word you say," the English Peer ejaculated and pushed him aside.

"He wants you to remove your shoes," someone explained.

"A lot of nonsense! I'll do nothing of the sort," the English Peer retorted. He looked round the mosque and left.

The party returned to a restaurant and sat outside drinking. While they did so the English Peer looked across the street.

"Why, there's the old josser who spoke to me in the mosque!" he exclaimed. "He obviously doesn't like me! If looks could kill . . ."

"Be careful he hasn't a knife," someone laughed.

Robert Hichens held up his hand.

"Don't," he begged, "don't laugh! It's not funny, the priest is putting a curse on you. It's a terrible one – I know of it."

"Good Lord! I don't believe that superstitious nonsense!"

The English Peer returned home.

The first disaster that happened was that his eldest son, a little boy of seven, was walking along the pavement with his Nanny when he ran into the road and was killed instantly by a lorry.

Next he heard that his wife, whom he loved, had been killed in an aeroplane crash. Thirdly a very dear friend had died in Paris.

The English Peer could not help connecting these overwhelming tragedies with the curse. He wrote to Robert Hichens, who by now was at his villa in the South of France, asking his help.

Robert Hichens crossed the Mediterranean and sought out the priest with the long beard. He begged him to take off the curse, offering, on the English Peer's instructions, any money he required to do so.

The priest shook his head.

"The curse must wear itself out!" was his reply.

1931

I am beginning to think about 'the World Behind the World', as the Chinese call it, instead of just 'feeling' it is there.

In the wind of the mountains and the song of the lowlands,
In the veil of night and the mists of dawn,
It is cried aloud that Thought alone
Was, Is, and Abides.

By chance – but does anything in life depend on chance? – I have just found *The Way of Power* by L. Adams Beck. In it I read:

"The Greeks and Romans both believed in the healing power of dreams, and in ancient Rome the College of the Inspired Dreams was a place of gathering for those who were sick or sad.

"It was dedicated to Aesculapius the Healer, and it was believed he was the inspirer of these dreams. Those needing help slept in the quiet of the sacred cloisters and seldom without result.

"One sees exactly why that should be and wish such help could be given now, and without human intervention, to those who need it.

"But it is a true saying that we can participate in heaven and its gifts only in so far as heaven is within ourselves.

"How can people empty of heaven realise the possibilities of dreams or the meaning of that little-known saying of Christ's:

45

"When the outside becomes the inside then the Kingdom of Heaven is come."

"It means that when for any man the deceptions and distortions of the outer world are swallowed up in realisation of the inner, the hidden world – when the outer and the submerged selves have joined hands and are one – then he has touched immortality and has drunk of the wine of eternal joy.

"It is a strange thought that all round us, hidden in every recurring night, lie these silent fields of harvest in which so few are reapers. Yet they lie, ripening in sunshine."

I have begun to read everything I can on Tibet, on Yoga and reincarnation. I found this verse and it meant something important to me:

Never the Spirit was born. The Spirit shall cease to be, never.
Never was time it was not. End and beginning are dreams.
Birthless and deathless and changeless abideth the Spirit for ever.
Death cannot touch it at all, dead though the house of it seems.

1931

London

I am suffering very painful colitis due to unhappiness and worry. I am told of a Temple of Healing where a friend of mine believes she had an inflamed appendix removed by spirit surgery.

It is near Olympia and when I arrived the house was dimly lit and there were pictures on every wall painted by artists in a trance. I did not of course say what was wrong with me.

I was taken to a room upstairs where the lights were blue and I lay down on a couch the length of a hospital bed. I was left alone for some time and then the door opened and a woman dressed in white and in a deep trance was led in by the attendants.

She stood beside me stretching out her arms, the fingers of each hand extended.

"My Guide tells me you have an inflammation in your body," the Medium said in a soft, far-away voice. "He can't operate, but says you must take a spoonful of olive oil three or four times a day."

She did not move and after a long pause she added:

"Healing rays have been poured into you and restoration has begun."

Then she was led from the room.

I did as I was told and the colitis became a little better, but not cured. So I got in touch with the well-known herbalist, Mrs. Layel at Culpeper.

Nicholas Culpeper was a famous astrologer-physician who lived in the 17th century. After a short apprenticeship to an apothecary in 1640 he set up his own practice in Spitalfields.

He left in his legacy to future generations a vast quantity of herbal remedies which are still as invaluable to-day as they were three hundred years ago.

I learn that sorrel will cure the blood, butcher's broom a headache; parsley and pimpernel will remove kidney trouble, borage inflammations.

I am convinced of the forgotten power of herbs and they have opened my eyes to the dangers of treatment by modern drugs, many of which have side-effects not envisaged when they were prescribed.

I learn that the Greeks had a great knowledge of herbs, so had the Romans, the Egyptians and of course the Chinese.

Addition: It was from Mrs. Layel I first heard of Ginseng, which the Chinese had for generations prescribed for vitality and eternal youth.

I had no idea then that years later it was to be so important to me personally and to the National Health Movement.

1932

I am very excited by a book Ronald has given me called: *A New Model of the Universe* by P. D. Ouspensky.

It tells me so much that I have wanted to know, so much that I do not yet understand:

On the first page I read:

All religion, all myths, all beliefs, all prophecies, heroic legends of all people and all countries, are based on the recognition of the existence sometime and somewhere of a knowledge far superior to the knowledge we possess.

Ouspensky also writes:

The idea of a knowledge which surpasses all ordinary human knowledge and is inaccessible to ordinary people, but which exists somewhere . . . permeates the whole bastion of the thoughts of mankind from the most remote periods.

This is what I have believed and what I want to know about.

This book stimulates thought and awakens awareness. For a long time I have been reading what I feel rather than the words in front of my eyes.

Often I will be thrilled, elated, made aware by what I have read, seeing pictures vividly and completely real; and then on re-reading the paragraph slowly, carefully, I find the words are very different from my first interpretation of them.

Our response to this compelling inspiration on the part of the author depends, I believe, on how far we, the readers have advanced in inner knowledge.

The books which stimulated and excited me as a child, like *The Princess and the Goblins* and *The Story of the Weathercock*, now seem quite ordinary little tales.

But when I first read them over and over again they took me through the Looking-Glass into that world of mystery and wonder which is always a little ahead of me.

> '. . . *how hold*
> *That glittering courage, or that soaring thought*
> *Which pierces through dissembling doubt*
> *Then dives—into a lake of live desire,*
> *Surrounded by the snow-capped mountains of the*
> *mind?*'

1932

Cap Ferrat
South of France

How alive and vivid faith can be is shown to us when it is concentrated within four walls.

Then we call it 'atmosphere', but it is really the life force concentrated by human beings within a confined space and absorbed by the porous quality of inanimate objects.

This, of course, explains how charms can in actual fact become lucky, how a picture, a flag or a book can become potent and perform miracles for those who draw from them some of the faith which has been concentrated in them by others.

To-day I experienced one of the most wonderful atmospheres I have ever known in the little church of St. Jean at Cap Ferrat which is attended only by the poor fisherfolk of the village.

I entered it one evening after dusk. The Church was in darkness save for a light hanging above the main altar which flickered in the shape of a cross.

I felt I was not alone but compassed about by a cloud of witnesses. God seemed very near.

Addition: This Church has now been completely changed and redecorated by Jean Cocteau and the atmosphere, the vividness of faith, has gone. It is warmly recommended in the Guide books!

1932

Bride les Bains
France

I have been ill with a bad throat and also from worrying over my divorce. My Doctor has insisted I should come here to Bride les Bains in France.

"Mountains and torrents are excellent for the mind," he said and he was right.

At night I hear the cascade of water falling down to the Valley from the white snows on the mountains, and in the day-time I climb up above the small town and look at the beautiful view.

To-day I was sitting in the sunshine with the Autumn crocus all round me and looking at the snowy peaks, when suddenly I had the strangest impression of peace.

It was as if everything ceased breathing and there was a complete and absolute silence. The world stood still and I knew it was 'the Peace of God which passes all understanding'.

When Ronald arrived to stay with me a week later I told him what had happened and he understood.

Addition: When I was in India in 1958, Ian and I went to Sarnath where Buddha preached his first sermon. I wandered away from my son who was listening to our guide and stood alone among the rocks and shrubs.

Suddenly I felt again that same overwhelming peace and absolute silence. It enveloped me and I felt as if I had ceased to breathe.

It passed all understanding but it was there.

India is so full of mystery and the miraculous. I wrote a poem to Buddhism which I felt so vividly at Sarnath.

> *The rustle of leaves in the banyan tree*
> *As it shelters the old men from the sun.*
> *Wood smoke and the smell of glee,*
> *White bullocks homeward come.*
> *Beauty and misery side by side,*
> *Famine and cholera, fear and strife.*
> *Yet underneath the mystic tide*
> *Of hope and faith which lifts each life*
> *Towards Nirvana.*

1932

I am practising Yoga breathing, and now I can often hear music when I listen and at night I have dreams which are vivid with colour and leave me with an intense feeling of happiness.

At the moment I am passing through a very difficult time in my life – I am depressed, unhappy and apprehensive, but when I dream everything is golden.

I have also seen pictures on the darkness when I lie in bed – usually of people but sometimes of views. They are about a foot square and I can't yet interpret them.

The Garden of Vision, another of Adam Beck's books, has taught me the rules of the World Behind the World and I repeat it to myself.

> *I have no parents; I make the heaven and the earth my parents.*
> *I have no home; I make my innermost my home.*
> *I have no magic power; I make the Self my power.*
> *I have no miracles; I make the righteous Law my miracle.*
> *I have no sword; I make that state which is above and beyond reason my sword.*

1933

Baden-Baden
Germany

I am at Dr. Douglas's Sanatorium in Baden-Baden, which is the fashionable resort of the very rich who over-eat. The Doctor's great interest is in the results of his experiments with olive oil on liver complaints.

I have colitis and while he cures me he shows me his successes with sclerosis of the liver.

I remember that I was told at the Temple of Healing that I needed oil and realise the medium was right.

Another patient is Dr. Frank Buchmann an American who inaugurated the Oxford Group Movement which had an amazing success in the '20s. After a Vision of the Cross in England in 1908 he believes he has discovered within himself a new power.

He began to change the lives of his friends. House-parties were arranged all over England where he spoke and those present 'shared' their sins.

The Group started in the English Universities but extended their message to industries and coal mines.

Their aims were:

Absolute poverty
Absolute purity
Absolute unselfishness
Absolute love.

The Marquess of Salisbury – one of the most influen-tial men in Britain – is one of Dr. Buchmann's supporters. When asked why, he replied:

"It is the Spirit moving on the water, and I dare not stand aside."

Criticism abounds because in surrendering themselves to the Movement the Groups are also asked to surrender their money. Moreover they publish no accounts and when asked why when travelling they stayed in 'posh' hotels Dr. Buchmann replied:

"Why shouldn't we stay in posh hotels? Isn't God a millionaire?"

I ask Dr. Buchmann to hold a meeting at the Sanatorium in the evening so that we can ask him questions. He is rather reluctant but I press him and he agrees.

About 30 people attend. Dr. Buchmann is stocky, stout and benevolent-looking, with thin smiling lips and bright eyes behind gold-rimmed spectacles.

One would guess him to be a Bank Manager. We ask several questions which he answers accurately but uninspiringly. It is difficult to understand why he has had such success.

His enemies are violently opposed to the Movement. A fellow and tutor of an Oxford College has written:

"I have known Oxford for 3 years as an undergraduate and I have worked in Oxford as a College Tutor for some 22 years, it seems to me that of all the movements, almost if not quite the most depraved in its attitude, tending to be most insidiously inimical to the formation of fine character, is the Group Movement which Dr. Buchmann has brought us from America."

Yet thousands of people including Royalty like Queen Marie of Roumania, the ex-King of Greece, and the King of Spain followed him in admiration.

I wanted to feel the vivid spark which he ignited in them. I felt nothing.

As the meeting broke up a friend with me said:

"Wouldn't it be awful if when we get to Heaven we find Frank Buchmann is God."

1933

Baden-Baden
Germany

While in Baden-Baden I have made a very interesting experiment. Staying with me is a friend, Eily Donald who has once been a professional Medium.

She is very clairvoyant and has frequently dreamed of the winners of famous horse-races like the Grand National.

To amuse ourselves we do automatic writing. She has a contact called Bertie. I say to him:

"If you are genuine, prove it by letting us win at Roulette."

"All right," he replies. "Go this evening to the Casino and play at six o'clock at the table near the window and I will tell you what number will win. But you are only to put on two marks (about 2*s*/-) and may not accumulate."

We did as he told us. Eily stood near the roulette wheel and I had the money ready. She was sure she would not know what the number was until the ball was rolling.

She said a number, I put on the two marks and the money was lost.

Baden-Baden is the only Casino I know which has a clock in the gambling rooms. Looking up I saw it was not exactly six o'clock.

We tried again.

Eily gave the right numbers ten times, then suddenly she said,

"It has gone – I can't do any more."

No-one whom I know or have heard of has ever been able to win ten times at roulette *en plein*.

We were paid thirty-five marks to one on each number and Eily covered her fare from England and some of her expenses in the Clinic.

1933

Vienna
Austria

This August Ronald and I are in Austria. He chose the place and we both saved all the year that we might have a holiday together.

When we awoke in the Arlberg-Orient express a bright clear sky was the background for snowy peaks, and in the valleys through which we were passing tiny chalets were painted with colours as brilliant as the sky and the flowers which filled every window-box.

We had our first glimpse of the wide, slow-flowing Danube and the great monastery at Melk standing on a sheer rock hundreds of feet above the little town.

Everywhere there was the deep mysterious green of fir trees and the silver of lake and river where golden youths and girls bathed and sang.

I shall never forget arriving in Vienna and driving through the streets in an open taxi.

It is love at first sight and we are both struck by the dignity and beauty of the city which had never become tawdry, although it was shabby from poverty and privation.

The Hotel Meissl und Schadn is like some caravanserai of eighteenth-century romance. Our rooms are enormous: they must have been used by the Arch-duke himself, we told each other.

In one corner of my bedroom is a huge, blue-tiled stove for use in cold weather, the walls are hung with icons and the sheets are buttoned over the blankets to make a kind of thin counterpane which cannot be tucked in.

The rooms are filled with the fragrance of fresh carnations which Ronald had ordered for me as a surprise.

I wish I could describe adequately the loveliness of Vienna. But really I have no words for the city or for its Cathedral – the Stephans-Dom – which has the most moving atmosphere of any place I have ever visited.

Here Ronald and I felt we had found the spirit of Vienna.

As we sat in an old carved pew looking towards the magnificent black altar, the nave in the solemn twilight seemed possessed of some mystic personality. Here Vienna's people had brought their hearts, broken by war and the aftermath of famine.

We both had an impression of hope tragically near to annihilation, yet remaining faithful because without it there was a hopelessness beyond all comprehension.

While we sat there yesterday watching all sorts and conditions of people come to pray before a miraculous picture, the light of many candles burning in the Chapel of the Immaculate Conception and flickering on the massive gold chandeliers hanging from the carved and painted roof, I saw the figure of a Cardinal.

He was outlined against the dark stone of the Cathedral so clearly as to show his features and the expression on his face.

It was deeply lined with suffering, but he had an expression of serenity and compassion, of faith transcending all the cruelties, the bestialities and the stupidities of mankind.

He remained with me for a long while.

1933

Austria

Seeboden is a small village on the banks of a warm lake in Carinthia. We had planned to go to Millstatt, a larger place, but when we arrived we thought it too big and crowded.

We hired a taxi and eventually found Seeboden, our task complicated by the fact that we speak no German and hardly any one knew a word of English.

Attached to a villa we saw a little wooden chalet. We were determined it should be ours. Rooms in Austria are let by the bed – the idea, therefore, being to pack as many beds as possible in a room.

Being a poor people they think nothing of sharing. In the villa, for instance, a judge, his wife and their three children, all over fifteen, shared a room together.

When Ronald and I asked for a whole room each they simply could not understand our wild extravagance.

"You want one room – two beds, yes?" they would insist.

Finally, by bribery and corruption we obtained the chalet, which had a room downstairs with a balcony overlooking the lake, a room upstairs, and – joy of joys! – a private lavatory.

The top room had been taken by a so-called 'engaged couple' who moved with the uttermost good humour into the boathouse, where on wet nights they sleep with an umbrella over their heads since the roof leaks.

The Austrians are a delightful people, so kind and so good-natured as almost to make one want to shake them and tell them to stick up for their rights.

We eat at a café on the lakeside while a band plays and where the chief dishes are young deer shot in the surrounding forests and *wilden beeren* (wild strawberries).

We have these too, for breakfast every morning with hot rolls and a huge jug of steaming coffee served with great spoonfuls of whipped cream.

The mornings we spend bathing and sunbathing, watching with amusement the guests at the villa come down to the lake with cakes of soap and wash themselves.

In the afternoons we walk up the steep sides of the mountains, finding attractive little villages where the coffee is beyond praise and where the church is always beautiful.

The wood carving over the altars and on the pulpits is often coloured but always in perfect taste. We never see anything tawdry or even ugly in these ancient buildings.

We find too, it is easy to pray in them; the faithful who have worshipped there for generations have left a living impression of the God they loved.

Then, as the sun sinks and we feel the cold, chill air from the distant snows, we hurry home passing Calvaries and lowing cattle, to the welcoming lights and music of the lakeside cafes.

One day as we walk round the lake we are caught in a thunderstorm; the beating rain, blinding flashes of lightning and the tempestuous waves are really quite terrifying. Then, as suddenly as it had arisen, the storm subsides and the sun shines on the rain-washed country with a dazzling brilliance.

As we hurry home to change our soaked clothes we see on the other side of the lake the most magnificent Castle. It is white with a black roof surmounted by a flag floating in the breeze.

Against the background of green hills, rising until in the distance one can see the white peaks shimmering against the blue sky, it is lovely beyond words.

It has, too an enchantment, as if the fairy palaces one dreamt of in the nursery have come to life.

"I must go there," I tell Ronald. "I want to see the inside of an Austrian Castle for my new book."

We sit on a seat to look at it.

"I'm afraid as the flag is flying," I remark, "the Herr Baron himself is in residence."

"We can but try to get in," Ronald said. "We'll go there to-morrow."

The next afternoon we set off. We can't find the Castle. The following day we try again and to-day we eventually discover it – in ruins!

There were Gothic archways, the remains of a tower, the foundations of a great courtyard, the first steps of a twisting staircase. No wall was more than eight feet tall, all being of grey, crumbly stone covered with moss and ivy.

How had we seen for over an hour the previous afternoon the Castle as it had once been in all its splendour?

1934

Kings Norton
Birmingham

Ronald is a prospective Parliamentary Candidate for the Kings Norton Division of Birmingham. It has been a Socialist seat for many years, but he hoped to win it for the Conservatives.

At his adoption meeting he made this inspired speech which moved everyone who heard it.

"Our philosophy, as Unionists, rests on the belief that a man's life in this world is a preparation for the next; that the soul of man is more important than his body; and that as far as is possible in the state of society in which he lives a man should be allowed to work out his destiny in his own way.

"We have our ideals; but ideals, we say if they are to have a real influence in our lives must be related – closely related – to the world in which we dwell now.

"We live in the world as it is; we strive to better it; but we realise that the Kingdom of God is above and it is man's soul that will attain to it – not man's body.

"No Government can change men's souls.

"As individuals our duty is to harmonise our own personal search for God with the need for living in the world with other men, and doing what we can to help them.

"As a Government our duty is to harmonise the personal development of each individual in the nation with the spiritual growth of the nation as a whole.

"We believe in the divine purpose in life. We think that every man and every woman has something to add to the stream of a nation's life; and every nation has its particular part to play with the other nations of the world in the general advance of mankind.

"As persons, as nations, we have different talents, different characters.

"Taken all together they make up the whole complete pattern of life – as many shades go to the making of a single colour.

"Our duty, we say, is to develop our own nation – the nation to which only by God's will, remember, we belong – and thus to make our fullest contribution to man's general progress.

"These are our principles.

"We have no cut and dried programme – 'no complicated abstract plan of life', as Browning says. So long as it agrees with the general principles we will put anything into practice. The only criterion is the national well-being.

"As for methods, we ask where does the balance of advantage lie? Hence our support of private enterprise and private ownership, and along with them, State-managed and State-owned concerns.

"As for the time factor – the balance of advantage to be settled then is between the claims of the immediate present and our duties as guardians for the future.

"You cannot explain faith. You cannot analyse it or dissect it. You can't really argue about it. It is within you – or it is not.

"In this uncertain, dangerous, difficult world I am certain of only two things; my faith in God and my faith in the English people.

"There is an instinct in us – our greatest heritage – for what is right and for what is noble. In times of trouble and in times of happiness it has never failed us.

"We have so much to be thankful for, so much to do. God grant that you and I – and England – will never fail."

1934

All religions are but crutches to help us, and all religions which uplift the mind and raise the spiritual standard of those who follow them must of necessity be good.

If it makes me a finer person and a better citizen to follow the rules of the Oxford Group or the Seventh Day Adventists, what does it matter to anyone else?

What each man and woman must decide for themselves is which pair of crutches fits them best, or – if you prefer it – which road leads to Rome the quickest.

All religion leads us eventually to God; the freedom of choice is ours, but to every man there comes at some time in his life a revelation and an awareness of the Spirit.

It may show itself in a conventional way, a sudden call to worship in one of the more orthodox religions, the scratching of a pencil in an Oxford Grouper's quiet time; it may be a light, a sense of God's presence in the most unlikely place.

Lord Marchwood who has sailed in the old windjammers, gone through the Singapore Mutiny, and been shipwrecked several times, has told me how, on a golf course, he had a sudden vision.

It came to him in a flash of light, a sense of unity with all creation. How long this moment lasted he had no idea, he only knew that when the light faded his partner had no inkling of what had occurred and without comment he went on with his game.

1934

London

Ronald and I have talked so often of the Divine power from which we can all draw strength and inspiration.

Ronald told me how the Greeks believed that it came through the solar plexus and they portrayed it as rays of fire.

The Christians later adopted this and their saints first had flames coming from that part of their body, then from their heads which became the halo.

Ronald draws on this power when he speaks and at first, because he is a positive speaker, he uses it too strongly.

I watched the front row of his audience bend like leaves as if blown by a gale force wind and I have spoken to him about it.

"You must control the power," I said. "You are blasting people out of their seats – it will frighten them."

I am also able to use the power although I have not Ronald's vision or his strong vibrations.

He has taught me that I must never make a speech without praying before I do so that it will help someone. And I must *always*, whatever my subject, give the members of the audience something to take away.

It is advice I intend to follow all my life.

1935

Bombay
India

My Uncle, Major General Sir John Scobell is G.O.C. (General Officer Commanding) of Bombay. He and his wife left on a tour of the troops and on the way they stopped to look at a Temple.

An Indian hurried up at their approach and asked if he could show them round but my uncle refused as he disliked guides. The man tried to insist but my Uncle swept him aside.

When they left the Temple Lady Scobell looked back and said:

"That man is staring at us in a most ferocious manner. I have a feeling he is cursing us."

My uncle only laughed but when they arrived at their destination they found that a trunk holding all their most valuable things had apparently fallen off the back of the car, although it had been very strongly tied there.

The next day my Uncle found that a gold watch he prized because it had belonged to his father, was missing and there seemed to be no possible way it could have been stolen.

Finally when they returned to Bombay they found a cable from my mother saying their only son and heir who was in England had died of Hodgkin's disease.

Addition: It seems unlikely that there could be any connection between the curse and George's death as he had been suffering from this incurable disease for some time. Yet the coincidence is there and my Uncle and Aunt were not only heartbroken but it also meant that their branch of the family was finished.

The Scobells or Scobahulls of Devon are one of the oldest Saxon families in Great Britain.

1935

London

Someone I loved very deeply has died. – I can't believe I will never see him again, never hear his laugh, never touch his hand. But I am grateful that I had so much. No-one can take that away.

"THOSE HOURS ARE MINE"

I am so happy that we had those days,
Wind in our faces, and a cloudless sky.
I am so happy that we had those nights,
Do you remember how the moonlight made you sigh?
Every note I hear, each shaft of sun,
Reminds me of something we have done.
Music which echoes down the years,
Music of laughter with a touch of tears.
Your hand in mine, the times we talked together,
Those hours are mine, for ever and for ever.

1936

I have just published a book called *The Forgotten City*.

The background to the story is that there is a forgotten city in us all, that the progression which each individual seeks is not in the future but in the past.

That spiritually one should look backwards not forwards, seeking a resurrection of the knowledge of God within us which is not to be acquired but rediscovered.

While I was writing it, I saw quite clearly a red brick Elizabethan wall mellowed by time and growing in front of it a number of Madonna lilies.

These lines were spoken in my mind:

> *'Twas Summer, and the honey-laden bees*
> *Hummed from the tall Annunciation flowers*
> *Which held in Gabriel's hand*
> *First came to earth*
> *To visit her, whose purity and faith*
> *Could find no equal in the House of God,*
> *And so became in very truth a Home*
> *For God Himself.*
> *Pale symbol of that beauty*
> *Lilies stood*
> *Yielding their fragrant treasure to the thieves . . .*

1936

Paris

I have married for the second time.

Two days ago on December 28th I married Hugh, a cousin of my first husband.

He had loved me for eight years, but it was difficult to decide whether we should get married because – with the exception of his mother – I did not like his family, and they did not like me. But finally we knew we could never be happy without each other.

On the morning of my wedding I received a letter from my brother Ronald which I knew I would treasure all my life.

"Darling, I must send you this morning all my love and thoughts and good wishes for the future. You know what you have meant to me these last five years – much more than I can ever hope to tell you – support, inspiration courage, faith and love – I've sought them from you often, never in vain.

"Now after to-day, it can't be quite the same – our relationship. But I'm not unhappy about it. I'm glad. Because I know you are doing the *right* thing, the wise thing, and the thing that is going to make you happier and even more lovable to all of us in the future.

"Darling, I'd hate you to marry any one but Hugh. I am genuinely delighted that after all this long time you are going to marry him. I can't think of any one I've met who will look after you and care for you as he will.

"Don't ever lose the memory of these last few years – the struggles as well as the victories – and don't forget darling, all the happy hours we've spent together. I don't think they're finished. There are many more for us in the future.

"But I want you to know that after them all and because of them I can say you've earned all the love and happiness there is for ever. I know that by marrying Hugh love and happiness will be yours more and more.

Bless you both – always.
"R".

Hugh and I wished to be married very quietly without any publicity – a difficult thing to do as I was always in the news and my divorce in 1933 had made headlines.

Because it was Christmas time we arranged to be married very early in the morning, first at the Guildhall, and there were no reporters, no photographers.

Then we had a Service of Blessing which was exactly the same as the Wedding Ceremony in the prayer book, at the Church of St. Ethelburgh the Virgin, in Bishopsgate.

It is a very old, very lovely Church, decorated with the Christmas flowers, and with no one present except Ronald and Hugh's best man it was to us both a very moving, very spiritual experience. I knew our marriage, whatever the difficulties ahead, would be a success.

We had planned to fly to Paris but there was a fog and the airport was closed. So instead we drove to Victoria Station.

Because McCorquodale prints for the Railways, we were able at this eleventh hour to get a coupe in the train to Dover, a private cabin on the cross-channel steamer and another coupe on the Golden Arrow to Paris.

I am aware now that fate is helping me at a very important moment in my life.

Hugh and I talked together as we travelled alone and we were caught up into an ecstasy which was divinely inspired.

73

Because of those hours together all the hesitations, anxieties and apprehensions which had surrounded us were swept away.

We became one as the Sacrament of marriage intended and our love is deeper and part of God.

London

I have published a small book on my philosophy, called *Touch the Stars*. In it I have tried to write down my thoughts on life and some of the ideas which I have discussed with Ronald.

I say in a foreword that I have put on paper what I believe to be the truth and the most helpful 'Way of Life'. I go on:

"Man has evolved, during his development from the ape-man to the civilised man, a brain.

"An ape can think up to a point, but he cannot remember last week's dinner, or plan Tuesday's luncheon and, most important of all, he has no desire to improve himself.

"Man instinctively wants to grow, to be greater, to be divine.

"There can be no denying the fact that primitive man tried to better himself, and that in the most primeval humans there is the instinct to develop.

"Man has always sought for something better and higher than himself.

"He has created God in his own image, and contrariwise believes that he is created in God's, merely so that this instinct of his should be satisfied, an instinct which continually demands from him one thing – progression!

"Between the ape-man and the human man there is the greatest factor in the whole development of civilisation, the instinct to be divine!

"This instinct has never been properly developed by

man himself: he is acutely conscious of it, but he is unaware of its tremendous power, not only over him personally, but over the whole Universe.

"Without this divine instinct, which the Church rather inadequately terms a soul, man would remain an ape with a brain.

"It is the spur, the prod which drives him mentally onwards, and induces him to set a standard for himself, always a step higher than that which he has as yet attained."

1935

London

Also in my book of philosophy I relate a well-known Tibetan legend which, translated, says:

> *Where there is faith*
> *Even the tooth of a dog*
> *Will admit light.*

The story is that an old woman who lived on the borders of the holy land (the sacred territory) asked her son who was journeying to Tibet on business to bring back with him a relic of some saintly Lama.

The son forgot, and the next year when he again made his journey his mother pleaded that he would remember her request. But his memory was fickle and the third year with tears his mother, who was getting old, begged him not to fail her.

This time, just as the caravan was wending its way over the stony, barren land homewards, the man remembered.

Ashamed to face his mother empty-handed, he saw the skull of a dog lying on the wayside and, ripping a tooth from the jaw, he carried it home in triumph.

"The tooth of a great and holy man," he told his delighted parent, who reverently laid it in an honourable position in her home, offering it adoration and prayer day after day.

News of the holy relic spread around, legends grew up about the enshrined tooth until people came from near and far to worship, journeying hundreds of miles over the bleak countryside to show their reverence for such a wonder.

Then suddenly one day from the tooth came a blue light and a mystic and spiritual aura surrounding the relic.

The concentrated faith of the worshippers had made the tooth of a dog holy but the holiness had come from them.

This is, I believe, to be the explanation of why so many relics of saints, holy pictures in Churches and Medallions can work miracles.

We pour into them particles of life from ourselves, which accumulate until they are powerful enough for us to draw on them.

"THE LEAPING FLAME"

> And there are those
> Through whom the stream flows slowly,
> Often dim and grey, but never still.
> Its flow unceasing, ceaseless,
> Till—as dawn breaks in a sable sky—
> The purpose of its moving stands revealed,
> The path of God—the leaping flame of life.

1936

London

This June Ronald decided that he must see for himself the conditions in the distressed areas of South Wales.

He started on a tour of Maes-teg, Merthyr Tydfil, Aberdare, Ebbw Vale, Dowlais, Maes-yr-haf, and parts of the Rhondda Valley.

In the details of his visit he was helped by the National Council of Social Service, while a cousin, Captain Geoffrey Crawshay who was District Commissioner for South Wales, arranged meetings for him with leaders of industry and Trades Union representatives.

Ronald has returned from this tour sickened and horrified by what he has seen. He says to me:

"I don't believe any one can realise how bad conditions are in the depressed areas until they have seen them for themselves. Equally I don't believe any one could realise the courageous fortitude of the people in these South Wales areas in face of great difficulties."

He was particularly struck by the character and outlook of the people, but in one market place he saw over 300 men sitting around doing nothing. In the centre someone was giving a religious address, but no-one paid the slightest attention.

Those men were too despondent to be interested in anything – they were not even Communists.

This scene remains in Ronald's mind indelibly; he refers to it again and again; the pathos of it is to him a physical hurt.

It also strengthened his hatred of injustice. He impresses on me over and over again how we must fight against it.

1937

London

My mother and I have been very worried this year because my younger brother Tony has had an accident.

He is twenty-three and over six feet four inches tall. Very good looking and extremely attractive with great charm, he has a delightfully unspoilt nature which makes him popular wherever he goes.

He has been A.D.C. to the G.O.C. (General Officer Commanding) in Egypt. But one day when he was riding with the General in Cairo, the ground having been watered was damp and greasy.

His horse slipped and threw him, and he landed on his head. He was taken unconscious to the hospital where he stayed for a month.

They couldn't find out what was wrong with him and he was brought back to England as a stretcher case. My mother went to meet him at Millbank Hospital when he arrived in March, to find him absolutely exhausted as owing to a muddle at Southampton he had been taken first to Netley Hospital and then sent on to London.

There were more muddles at Millbank: Tony arrived on Wednesday in Easter Week, and though he was listed as an urgent case, he was not examined on arrival.

Ronald was furious and, as he knew Alfred Duff Cooper, the Minister of War, who had been very nice to him in the House of Commons, he rang up the War Office and told him how Tony was being, in his opinion, neglected because the doctors were away for the holiday.

On the Tuesday after Easter four doctors examined

Tony, but they all failed to find out what was wrong with him.

He felt very ill, giddy and sick, his eyes were out of focus, and although the medical authorities kept saying he would get all right with rest, we weren't satisfied.

Tony was also depressed and miserable in Millbank, where everything was very old-fashioned and some of the hospital equipment was marked 1870!

My mother asked if she could take him to a nursing-home at Eastbourne, but, though it was thought to be a good idea, Tony was not well enough to be moved until the end of April.

She had fortunately insured both Ronald and Tony against accidents and the Company paid for him.

The 'Esperance' is a lovely nursing home in what had once been a private house, and it is run by Roman Catholic nuns. The atmosphere is peaceful and happy. The nuns, sweet-faced and sympathetic, told my mother not to worry.

"We'll get your son well," they said. "We will pray for him as well as nurse him and you will see how quickly his health will improve."

It does indeed seem a miracle how Tony started to get better from the moment he arrived at the "Esperance".

The very first night, after being very sick in the ambulance, he slept peacefully and the next day the doctor examined his neck and found, what had never been discovered before, that in falling from his horse he had nearly severed his spine at the base of his neck.

This was the reason his eyes were out of focus and he suffered from such bad headaches. They started electrical treatment at once and Tony has begun to look like himself again.

My mother is convinced his recovery was due to prayer.

1937

London

I have a son!

It is the most exciting, wonderful thing that has ever happened to me. Hugh and I have longed for one and I knew he would be beautiful, clever and loving.

I am a tremendous believer in prenatal influence. The Ancient Greeks always had fine statues round the room where their women gave birth, so that the children would be born beautiful.

I think a mother influences her child from the very moment of conception. I think too that how it is conceived is of paramount importance.

If the union of physical and spiritual love evokes in the actual act of conception the ecstasy which is as near as we get to the Divine – then the child will be beautiful.

This is proved over and over again by 'love children'.

Some Ancient Greeks believed that one could only learn through a body, and that before a baby quickened its mother went to a place where all the souls who wished to be reborn were waiting.

There a soul entered the embryo in her body.

When I was carrying my daughter, Raine, I was determined she should be beautiful and I not only looked at beauty but thought it.

I would never read a book or watch a film which I thought could induce in me wrong or bad thoughts and might affect my unborn child.

When Raine was born, I was unable to have an anaesthetic and she had the cord round her neck. It took three-quarters of an hour to make her breathe.

But she was meant to live and was so lovely that everyone who saw her exclaimed at her appearance.

I had looked at a picture of an ideal baby all the months she was on the way. My first visitors saw it and as the resemblance was so extraordinary they exclaimed: "You had her painted already!"

I was certain this time I should have a boy. I wanted him to be beautiful and also prayed and willed him to be brave and clever, to love people and hate injustice.

Addition: Ian was so beautiful as a little boy and looked so like an angel that I was afraid he would die. He had ash-blonde hair and a spiritual look that was very noticeable.

He grew up to be very clever, charming, a good mixer with every sort and kind of people, and with a *joie de vivre* which creates happiness wherever he goes.

Raine was acclaimed the most beautiful débutante of the year and later one of the most beautiful women in Great Britain.

1937

London

Gradually with Ronald's help I am finding my way through the Looking-Glass. Now at least I know what I believe and what I hope to find.

The following words are not mine but were written by someone who had found 'The Way'. The book came into my hand – not by chance, for nothing important in life is by chance – but because I longed for help and it was there.

"I believe that all the Universe is One of which we are a part.

"I believe that what we call 'Good' is undeveloped perfection and what we call 'Evil' is only undeveloped good.

"I believe that with fallible senses and brain we cannot attain to the knowledge of absolute truth, but that we sometimes have flashes of it which inspire and sustain us.

"I believe that Love, human and divine, is the prison-breaker of that prison of selfhood which confines and confuses us.

"I believe that for those who have attained enlightenment, super-normal (not super-human) powers are available to those who seek them.

"I believe our real prayer should be –

From the Unreal lead us to the Real;
From our blindness lead us to the light;
From evolution lead us to perfection.

84

Break down in us the prison of our false
    individuality and selfhood.
Unite us with the One who is in us and of
    Whom we are a part.
Teach us to rejoice in our own nobility and
    to recognise our
Divinity, that in blindness we may never sin
    against our true self.

The way is open to all, and all will eventually walk
in it."

1939

London

I have brought out a novel with the story based on re-incarnation. I feel so strongly that this is a true doctrine which Ronald and I have discussed so often.

It is the only reasonable explanation for the fact that Mozart could play the violin perfectly at the age of four, and it is the only *just* explanation for life in this the 3rd dimension.

When I was writing this novel I was 'helped' with it and everything fell into place.

My father had been a friend of Rudyard Kipling and I read *Kim* because of that and found it gave me something no other book had ever given me.

As I read it the pictures I saw in my mind were so vivid, so real that it was hard to understand how the actual words of the book could create them.

Later I read Kipling's poem:

> *They will come, come back again*
> *As long as the red earth rolls.*
> *He never wasted a leaf or tree,*
> *Do you think he would squander souls?*

It moved me, it told me what I wanted to know but I could not say that I had any real indication of my own previous incarnations.

I wanted to say with Rossetti:

> *I have been here before*
> *But where or how I cannot tell;*

I know the grass beyond the door,
The sweet keen smell,
The sighing sound; the lights around
the shore.

Instead I have met several people in my life who I am convinced I have "known" before.

"REUNION"

I saw you look at me and knew
This was the moment I had sought,
And sought in vain—yes, it was true
That love could happen swift as thought,
I didn't know your name.

I saw your eyes look into mine,
My heart was beating, did you know?
We passed through centuries of time,
But there was nothing now to show
We'd loved in other lives.

Something flashed from me to you.
You were trembling, so was I.
We didn't speak and yet we knew
That everything we felt was true
Because we'd met again.

1939

Caister-on-Sea

I am having a baby, so we have taken a house on the beach at Caister-on-Sea. The house was struck by lightning the night we arrived.

Ronald arrives to tell me of his sensational speech in the House of Commons on August 2nd which has filled the newspapers and stunned his constituents.

He accused the Prime Minister, Mr. Neville Chamberlain, of making – "jeering, pettifogging party speeches which divide the nation . . . when we are in a situation where within a month we, the young men of this country, may be going to fight, we may be going to die."

He was convinced that we were on the brink of war. As he talks so vividly and vitally, I have the inescapable conviction that the sands are running out. I am afraid.

Addition: Later when people spoke of his speech they said, "I was there, it was not just what he said, it was the way he said it." I knew exactly what had happened, the power had been too strong. This time the Members of Parliament had been blasted out of their seats.

Ronald was wrong by one day. On Sunday September 3rd, exactly one month and one day after his prophetic words in the House of Commons, we were at war with Germany.

He was killed eight months later.

1939

On leave from the Worcestershire Yeomanry Ronald shows me a letter he has written to someone who has asked him why a "kind, and just God" should permit so much suffering:

"Surely Evil and Good each exist because of the other. If Evil disappeared, Good too would cease to be. God did not create Good and Evil. He created Spirit or freedom.

"Man has created Good and Evil because of his inability to realise the Spirit – is a road to salvation, i.e., to the attainment of Spirit.

"There is a purpose in suffering – that we should try and spiritualise it – and ourselves through it. We should equally attempt to overcome it.

"Suffering is part of the freedom of life – as is Good and Evil, and Joy and Misery. Justice and Injustice cease to have any meaning if you disregard their human implications.

"Is this an answer to you? To pray for 'physical things' is merely to show yourself bound by things of the earth rather than of the Spirit."

The Christian life as Ronald sees it is a living, working philosophy, controlled and guided by the Great Creative Force of which he is always acutely conscious.

1940

Six Mile Bottom
Nr. Newmarket

My second son, Glen, was born last night at ten minutes to midnight on December 31st 1939.

There is three foot of snow on the ground and here we are nine miles from Cambridge where the Specialist who attended me lives.

I had prayed for another boy and when he arrived I had, as with my other children, a very difficult confinement, but I was ecstatic in knowing I had a second son.

Glen is a very large, solemn-looking baby and I am sure he has been reincarnated many times . . .

Addition: So many people have said to me since, that Glen is an old soul. He has an appreciation and knowledge of art and of all that is ancient and beautiful. He is unfailingly kind, especially to old people and to me. His personality develops year by year.

1940

France

In a letter Ronald, who was with the British Expeditionary Force in France wrote to someone who was groping for the truth, he said:

"You talked to me of prayer. That's the only thing that matters. I know that *now*, if I wasn't sure of it before.

"I'm also sure of this – that buildings and orthodoxy, or the embodiments of orthodoxy, churches, services and so on, are of immeasurable assistance.

"When they are cut off one at last realises their value. But how difficult it is to pray, as you say. Why? Because we've not learnt to contemplate – we're ignorant of how to meditate – without those two we can't pray.

"I feel it out here more and more. You at home do too because the war has smashed the armour of all our common lives. It is none the less a superb opportunity.

"Now is our chance to overcome what is probably sloth – our own unwillingness and incapacity to think afresh and *pray* afresh.

"Difficult? Of course. All real belief is. One has just got to persevere.

"Not that I can talk. I often think I fail in my ideals and aspirations. It's a comment on our lack of spiritual stamina.

"Butt it is what we must strive for; nationally and individually."

1940

Great Barford
Bedfordshire

Dunkirk is over, the British Expeditionary Force has by a miracle, been brought home by the little boats across the Channel . . . But some have not returned.

I shall remember those hot, dry, sunny days all my life. I was at our cottage in Bedfordshire. The lilac was in bloom, huge bushes of white, purple and mauve; the may trees were crimson and the blossom was heavy on the cherry trees.

Beyond the wattles which bordered the tiny lawn was the slow-moving, silver-grey river. Behind the cottage the gargoyles on the 15th century grey stone tower of the church stood sentinel at the end of the winding, sleepy little village.

It seemed to me that a great quiet lay over everything, as if the earth itself held its breath. I walked up and down the garden, waiting for the telephone to ring.

Every so often I could bear it no longer and would telephone my mother at Malvern.

"Have you heard anything, darling?"

"Nothing . . . I thought perhaps your ring . . ."

"I was afraid you might, but I had to speak to you . . . are you all right?"

"Of course!"

Her courage made one tremendously proud.

I went back to the garden. Moments from the past walked beside me.

Ronald as a little boy, playing at politics – making a speech – applauding himself.

Ronald and I walking through the shabby, dimly-lit

streets the first night we came to London – to stand awe-struck by the traffic and the impressiveness of the South Kensington Underground. Once again I could feel the tension of his fingers in mine, the throb in his voice, as he said, "I shall be Prime Minister . . ."

Ronald struggling . . . striving against poverty and illness . . . driven by a flame, consumed by his desire to fight injustice, to work for England . . .

His horror at the conditions in Shoreditch . . .

Ronald pale yet confident, making his speech before the Executive Committee of the King's Norton Association.

Ronald being carried shoulder high through the wet, slippery streets of Birmingham at one o'clock in the morning by the poorest and most loyal of his new constituents.

Ronald, slender, young, vital and dynamic, in an old, tired and very mature House of Commons.

Tony was there with me too. A little boy in a sailor suit, who couldn't pronounce his r's. The schoolboy, enthusiastic, happy and carefree – no reformer – an easy person to like, someone who was bound to be popular.

The second Lieutenant, so very tall, smart and gay . . .

I could hear his voice. He must have been about twenty. "I hope there's another war – if there isn't, I shall never be C.I.G.S." . . . A cry from my mother; "Don't talk like that, darling; you don't know what you're saying!"

Tony, 'the perfect A.D.C.', speaking affectionately of 'my General'. Tony in love – "She's marvellous, but . . . it's wonderful to be home, there's no one like one's own family."

Tony at Claridges that day we had lunched together in February, a red carnation in his buttonhole, a cigar between his fingers, and laughing gaily, still utterly care-free, at something which had amused us both.

Was that the telephone ? No, nothing breaks the silence in which even the river and the bees are muted . . .

The poppies are scarlet against the green of the poplars.

93

I look away from them, they remind me too vividly of Flanders poppies . . .

I remember hearing from my schoolmistress that my father had been killed. "You must be very brave, dear, for your mother's sake."

Ex-Servicemen, blinded and crippled, making poppies for a day of remembrance. A day? Well, at least we had kept the two minutes' silence!

Ronald, returning sick and ashamed from the Distressed Areas of South Wales . . .

"Did you do any good?"

"Only by showing them that a Tory M.P. can be human . . ."

His voice in the House:

"It is not generosity that the Welsh people want – it is justice."

"You can either do something or you can do nothing. If you are going to do something, you have got to spend money."

His quiet answer to the Whips who censured him for attacking his own party. "I must follow my own conscience."

Ronald, a year older, matured, but more clear-cut. The fire of truth, vision and strength of purpose in life, his conviction that this world is only a preparation for the next.

Ronald still fighting . . .

"It is the closed mind we must battle against."

". . . Though we may turn human beings into machines, we shall not in that way bring them happiness."

"Democracy can only survive if men believe in it more strongly than in dictatorship!"

Ronald speaking of England, looking from the top of the Malvern Hills over the fertile Severn Valley, Birmingham in the shadow, the sun lighting the tower of Worcester Cathedral.

"Our job is to do all we can to keep England great in a difficult world."

"Only through freedom can man find salvation."

"England, through the strength of her people, will conquer the tyranny of those who have set out to destroy the supreme values of life."

Ronald . . . yet more pictures of Ronald . . . and of Tony.

Persistent in my mind were Ronald's words the previous August:

"We are in a situation that within a month we may be going to fight; we may be going to die."

Had he been prophetic that moment in the House of Commons when a friend described him as 'defiant, faithful, devoted and brave beyond compare'?

I walk back up the garden; the sun is shining on the small casement windows under the thatch. Ronald helped to paint them when we first bought the cottage, and he had helped too, to scrape the old beams – ship's timbers.

I walk down again; soon the lilies will be out; the roses are already in bud. Ronald loved flowers; we had laughingly planned white lilies and crimson roses on our graves when we should be buried.

Once in Austria I had entered his room while he was asleep. He lay on his back, very straight and still . . . "a crusader on a tomb," I told him.

"That is how I shall be in Westminster Abbey."

He was so sure of his future. "Reforms can only come from the top. There is so much for me to do."

I walk again over the firm dry lawn.

The minutes pass slowly, so slowly that I feel as if a century of time has been lived since I last looked at the clock.

Now I remember the bitter moments; an unkind word; a needless criticism; times when I had been too busy; letters which had not been written; presents which had not been given.

Is there any hell like the hell of regretting when it is too late?

Was it too late? Was I to have my chance over again? Why had I not gone to see them at school more often?

95

Why had I not done more in the constituency? Why had I not sent them more presents to the Front? And money – we had always been so hard up – couldn't I have gone without more . . . for them?

Another chance, please God, another chance!

We had much, we three. A mother we adored and who adored us. A home where we were always happy. A devotion to each other which was rare. A sense of family which united 'us' against the world.

"There's no one like one's own family."

"No one could understand . . . except us."

"Let us just be alone . . . all together."

I remember Ronald talking to me on the soft sandy beach in Brittany.

"People are so ungrateful; they always want more; they never remember how much they have had already."

Was it greed to want more? Yet could I ever be sufficiently grateful for what I had had?

The love, the friendship, the understanding, the special interest in everything which concerned me and them, the development within myself because someone else believed me capable, not only of my best, but of so much more besides.

Isn't there a special word for that? Yes – 'faith'. That was what my generation had always been seeking – faith in ourselves. Faith! – their faith in me and mine in them.

"*And you ask*," Ronald had written, "*what do we want out of Life? That question should only be asked by you of yourself. It can be answered only by you. In other words – or written in a word – 'Faith'.*"

Whatever happened in the future, the past was mine – a past in which I had known and found faith – and having found it, would never lose it again.

What Ronald and Tony had given to me they would never take away.

Darkness fell . . . the telephone did not ring.

But to a woman waiting alone, in an empty home, came the tidings that both her sons were 'missing'.

1940

Great Barford
Bedfordshire

We are *home* again and I have never felt so relieved.

Immediately after Dunkirk I was invited to take my children to stay with a great friend in Canada. Raine is eight, Ian is three, Glen was then 5 months old and we had been told that babies were often killed by the blast of bombs.

Winston Churchill, now Prime Minister, had told his personal friends that to fight 'on the beaches' and to the death, he was prepared to evacuate all the women and children from the South of England.

A Government scheme was put in hand to take children overseas, to the Commonwealth and America.

We went to Canada – a terrifying journey with over 1,100 children on board and not enough life-boats. We were chased by a submarine and when we reached the Atlantic had no escort.

Soon after we arrived the *City of Benares* which was full of children was sunk and the Government scheme was closed down. I had arranged for any children who came from Ronald's Constituency to get in touch with me, but only 7,000 children altogether had got away from England.

I knew then I could not accept privilege in wartime for myself or my children. It was something Ronald would never have approved.

I demanded to go home. Unfortunately I had signed a paper on leaving England to say I would not return for six months.

However after some difficulty and by sheer determination I received a special permit to return on the last passenger ship leaving Montreal, which was to carry the first Empire Air Training Unit to England.

The warm-hearted Canadians were horrified at my decision to go home. They begged, argued and even abused me for undertaking such a dangerous journey and risking my children's lives.

I knew I was right and it was what Ronald would want me to do, but I began to have nightmares that Ian was drowning and I was helpless to save him!

Then I remembered how Winston Churchill had described in *The World Crisis* how, when in 1914 he was asked to become First Lord of the Admiralty, he opened the Bible at random and found encouragement and re-assurance from the verses on which his eyes fell.

One night I prayed for a long time; then I opened my Bible with my eyes shut and put my finger on a verse. It read:

"And there went a proclamation through the host about the going down of the sun, saying, 'Every man to his city, and every man to his own country'."

I knew then that I was doing the right thing; God would take care of us and we should arrive safely.

When we sailed in a blizzard we learnt that the *Graf Spey* was at large in the Atlantic and the crew of the ship in which we were travelling had seen the heroic fight of the *Jervis Bay* on the way over.

This small brave merchant-ship had fought the huge battle-ship to the death while the convoy she was escorting escaped to safety.

We had two guns which could only fire sideways between the funnels, no escort, and the sea was very rough.

I can't say I slept very much. One night I heard a terrific bang and thought, "Now we're for it!" I sprang out of bed, picked up Ian's snow suit, which was lying ready, and suddenly realised that it was very quiet – there were no bells or alarms.

I opened my cabin door and looked into the corridor; everything was as usual. I realised that it could only have been a door slamming overhead which had frightened me.

It was then that a feeling of sheer terror took possession of me: we were trapped, we had to go on and forward, whatever happened.

Anyone who has been in danger will understand my feelings at that moment – the agony of fear is horrible.

Then suddenly I knew, with an absolute certainty, that someone was with me – not Ronald, but someone I had once loved and who had loved me. He had been killed in a flying accident, but he had been a sailor. He was there as surely as if I could see and hear him.

He was beside me, as real and as unchanged in our relationship to each other as he had been when I had last seen him. I was no longer afraid, my fear vanished, and I knew with an unshakeable conviction that he had come to take us into port.

I fell asleep, but he was still there in the morning and for the rest of the voyage.

Only when we sighted the coast of England did he go as swiftly as he had come, and I have never been close to him since.

1941

January 4th

A letter received from Lieut. Derek Woodward, 209 Battery Worcestershire Yeomanry, British Prisoner of War OFLAG VII, Germany, says:

"All our guns were out of action and word had been given to make for the coast. On May 30th at about 8.30 a.m. we were about 20 miles from Cassel making our way about 2 miles east of Watou along a ditch bordering a lane, but we were not moving very fast as mist was rising and the country was getting open.

"Ronald called me forward. While with him we saw German tanks going into action against other troops half a mile ahead. We decided to conceal ourselves, but later three tanks converged on us and we had to get up. As Ronald rose he was hit in the head by a bullet and killed instantly. I was about five yards away with 50 men following. We were marched off immediately."

I didn't tell my mother at the time, but when Ronald was missing after Dunkirk I had a strange dream.

I dreamt I saw him with a round bullet hole in the centre of his forehead. He was very pale and did not speak when I spoke to him.

This letter is the first indication we have had that he was shot in the forehead.

I am writing down now another dream which I had later. It was so vivid! I was walking along a narrow path when Ronald came round the corner.

He was looking full of life and vitality, as he always did, and I rushed up to him to cry:

"Darling, you are alive! I knew you were, how wonderful!"

We turned and walked the way I had come. I said:

"Mummy will be thrilled and she has all your press cuttings. You will be so amused at all the marvellous things people said about you when they thought you were dead."

He laughed and while I am radiant with happiness I wake up.

I have written a poem about that dream.

"ALIVE"

I dreamt last night of you,
It was so real, so true, I knew
You lived – although they said
You were dead.

I dreamed you kissed me, then
We laughed, just as we did when
You were here – before they said
That you were dead.

I know now you are alive
I cannot see you but you are beside
Me still, as you were before they said –
So stupidly – that you were dead.

1941

"To Ronald"
Killed near Cassel, May 30, 1940

On the 'Dunkirk beaches' of England's story,
   She finds her soul and her greatest glory,
For the men who love her are always the same,
   Ready to die in freedom's name.

The vision that once our fathers knew
   Has been born again. Can we make it true?
So that out of the muddle and sins of the past
   England may find her peace at last?

1941

Bedfordshire

Once again my mother has had to go through the long drawn out agony of uncertainty. We know there is no longer any hope that Ronald is not dead but Tony is still missing.

My mother has written to every man in the Lincolnshire Regiment who has been taken prisoner. Several have replied that they have heard that Captain Anthony Cartland is a prisoner.

But she tortures herself wondering if he is wounded and too ill to write. She lies awake at night hearing the roar of the German aeroplanes overhead and praying he is not being badly treated.

I have seen a Medium who is absolutely certain that Tony is on 'the earth plain' so I suggest to my mother that she makes an appointment with Estelle Roberts a famous clairvoyant. She lives in Esher and my mother has telephoned her but called herself Mrs. Hamilton.

She has just telephoned me to describe how Estelle Roberts received her in a flower-filled sitting room with windows opening on the garden. They sat down in arm chairs opposite each other and talked for a moment or too about the weather. Suddenly Mrs. Roberts said:

"You have come to consult me about your sons – they are both here beside me."

"Not both," my mother said quietly. "One is a prisoner."

Estelle Roberts shook her head.

"No, they are together. The youngest one – he is wearing a button hole – tells me that he was killed the day

103

before his brother. Now they are both talking together; they have so much they want to say to you."

But my mother won't listen. She is sure that Tony is alive.

"What a waste of money!" she says to me now.

Addition: We learnt on February 7th, 1942 from the Minister of Defence, a great friend of Ronald's, that he had heard through the American Embassy that Tony was buried at Zuidschote, north of Ypres, and a letter from a prisoner-of-war gave the full details of his death:

"Left to hold the rearguard trench, he was surrounded and part of his Company were killed. The German officer asked the survivors to surrender – Tony's answer was to seize an automatic gun and open rapid fire.

"He was wounded and again asked to surrender. He replied:

"I will surrender only to God and fight to the last man and the last round."

He continued to fire from an automatic gun. He died shortly afterwards. Estelle Roberts had been right – Tony had been killed on May 29th, the day before Ronald.

1943

Bedfordshire

To-day I had driven half across the county to a search-light unit and on the way back I stopped my car.

It is spring and there were bluebells beneath the trees and primroses under the hedges. There was the soft 'coo' of the wood pigeons, otherwise there was a strange still-ness which made one listen as if for a note of music.

But after a few moments I forgot the present and slipped away into the past, remembering other springs when Ronald and I had walked across St. James's Park to admire the bulbs, and when the tulips in my mother's garden had been crimson beside the yellow daffodils.

Noel Coward had expressed it so well:

> *I'll see you again,*
> *Whenever spring breaks through again,*
> *Time may lie heavy between;*
> *But what has been*
> *Is past forgetting . . .*

I think I was humming to myself, when a quiet voice said:

"Could you please give me a lift?"

Startled, I turned my head to see a little old woman in grey. I really didn't notice much else about her because my eyes were full of tears.

"Yes, of course, get in," I answered, and she sat down beside me.

I started the car quickly, feeling guilty at having wasted so much time day-dreaming, when I should have been on my way home.

We drove in silence, which was unusual, because generally I found lots to say to anyone I picked up.

But what has been
Is past forgetting . . .

I suppose unconsciously I must have been humming again, for my companion said:

"And you wouldn't want to, would you?"

"Of course not!"

"Besides, what has been – is!"

I didn't reply because we were passing a convoy. When they were past she spoke again.

"We know that really; only sometimes we get muddled by time and feel unsure and afraid."

"Yes, afraid . . . that we will never see them again," I whispered.

"That's the winter," she said. "But there is always the spring to tell us the truth."

We had come to the summit of the hill beyond Ampthill, the misty-blue valley of the Ouse lay below us. The sun had come through the clouds and thrown ladders of living gold down towards the river.

It came to my mind that the valley must have looked much the same when the Romans came marching into the country, when it became the central kingdom of Mercia, when the Danes set up their camps and stockades, when the Normans held tournaments and when Oliver Cromwell came galloping through from the Fens.

The land had not changed. But what of those who had passed through it? A soft voice said beside me:

"Nothing is wasted – nothing is lost."

The beauty of the valley with its shafts of sunshine was suddenly breathtaking.

We drove down the hill; at the foot of it there was an ambulance and a little crowd of people. A military policeman held up his hand and came across to me.

"Are you going Cardington way, miss? A W.A.A.F. here has seen a man knocked down. She's not hurt herself, but it's given her a bit of a shock."

"I'll take her," I said, thinking how the needs of the

living must always intrude on thoughts of the dead . . .
no, I corrected myself . . . on those who had left us.

I looked across the road and saw the girl advance in
response to the M.P.'s beckoning hand. She looked pale
but quite composed. I smiled at her, then turned to my
passenger . . .

I was alone. The little woman in grey must have
slipped away while I was talking. I tried to see where she
had gone, but the spring sunshine dazzled my eyes.

1943

Bedfordshire

I have always believed that colour is important physiologically and especially to me. Since I grew up I had always had my bedroom with blue walls and red curtains.

When I first visited Luxor in Egypt I changed this to the brilliant turquoise blue of a scarab and the flame pink used in the tombs of the Kings.

In my opinion these colours help, inspire and activate those who use them, and yet no-one in the War Office seems to be aware of this.

Bedfordshire being in the centre of England is full of secret stations. I as the Chief – (and only) – Lady Welfare Officer for the Armed Services and the only outsider allowed into the most secret of them all.

A lovely old house and its grounds has been taken over by the R.A.F. and such 'hush-hush' things happen there that it must never be mentioned.

All I'm concerned with is the W.A.A.F. personnel. They are fed up with being confined there, and hardly feel they are in the war.

I am asked to do what I can about their morale but have no money. All the Welfare Office can supply are dartboards!

I know about what appealing for 'comforts for the troops' produces:— boring sermons, children's books and ghastly pictures! One was of a boned herring on a plate!

I have finally raised some money and persuaded the Officer Commanding to let me do up not only the restrooms but the huts in which the personnel work.

Needless to say everything is on coupons or unobtainable, but I managed to get cork-matting dyed flame colour for the floor, hessian the same red for the windows, and the walls painted a soft Adam green.

For pictures I have obtained some prewar railway posters from my husband's printing firm. I find that even "Come to Sunny Bournemouth" or "Ilfracombe for the Sands and Sea" looks nice and colourful in red-painted frames.

My Welfare General keeps barking at me: "A door is a door whatever colour you paint it." He is wrong! The morale at the 'hush-hush' station had gone up 100% and I have started on others.

At Leighton Buzzard we have a fighter group. They work in what looks like a small underground theatre. Over the whole area is camouflage netting.

The British Colour Council promptly painted the Operational Theatre in battle-ship grey. One can't imagine anything more depressing!

I have put in my colours of tnrquoise and flame and everyone looks and is much happier.

Addition: I have found years later that those who heal by colour believe that:

Turquoise – releases psychological passions, controls exhaling and is calming to nervous tension.
Red – stimulates, excites, activates.

1943

Great Barford
Bedfordshire

I heard last year that a friend of Ronald's was thinking of writing his biography. I was upset at the idea because I felt the man in question would never do Ronald justice.

I telephoned my mother and told her of my fears.

"But of course he mustn't write a book about Ronald," she said. "You must write one."

"I must?" I cried in consternation; "but I don't think I can."

"Of course you can," my mother answered. "Ronald will help you!"

I had never written a biography before. I expected it to be a formidable task. In fact it was the easiest book I have ever written. I had only to sit down with pen and paper for the book to be as it were dictated to me.

I finished this biography for which the Prime Minister, Winston Churchill, wrote the preface, in a month. I am convinced that Ronald helped me with this book, just as I am certain he helps me at other times and in so many ways.

Now it has been published and the reviews are fantastically warm and congratulatory.

I know that this book will inspire, help and guide many young men and perhaps carry on Ronald's crusade for the peace and prosperity of this country and for justice for everyone.

The Earl of Selborne who has compiled a symposium of Ronald's speeches has written in his foreword:

"Those who have read the life of Ronald Cartland will have realised the inestimable loss that his death has meant to England . . . His courage was remarkable. What is equally remarkable is the degree in which all the reforms he advocated have been adopted by the Conservative Party within a few years of his vainly urging them."

These words tell me that Ronald's vision will not be lost.

Addition: 1977. The Bishop of Southwark, Mervyn Stockwood, said when it was published that my biography of Ronald was a book which influenced him more than anything he had read for a long time.

A few days ago he re-confirmed that statement.

Peter Walker, a Member of Parliament who has held Cabinet Rank, has just written an article in a Birmingham newspaper saying:

"Looking at his remarkable speeches now one cannot help but reflect that had he lived he could well have been the present Conservative leader – maybe Prime Minister."

1944

Great Barford
Bedfordshire

The Marriage Service is, I think, a spiritual moment in every woman's life, and therefore the white dress, the veil, the coronet of orange blossom are all still of tremendous psychological importance.

However lightly young people may regard marriage to-day I believe the ceremony can inspire them and evoke the spiritual side of love which is often forgotten.

As the only female Welfare Officer in Bedfordshire, I am looking after an enormous number of W.A.A.F. personnel in dozens of secret stations.

They are very, very secret and the women get bored with never seeing an aeroplane, with never hearing a shot fired, and with feeling they are not really a part of the war effort.

Actually their work is of vital importance, but it is difficult to persuade them of this.

All they know is they are cooped up in 'hush-hush' stations, they see very few outsiders, except me, and they are fed up to the teeth with their uniform, their ugly underclothes and their flat-heeled clumping shoes.

It was obviously a man who decided the Services should only have twelve coupons a year with which to buy handkerchiefs! One can hardly imagine a more ludicrous idea of how a woman should spend those precious coupons.

And I am sure that because a man thought of it, it was agreed to by all those de-sexed, strident female Controllers (who thought of that title?) of whom we are all terrified, and who manage in some extraordinary way to make those of the same sex they command feel vaguely apologetic because they are women.

The girls all came crying to me that they could not possibly be married in anything but white.

"I've got to have a white wedding," they each insisted. "I wouldn't feel married otherwise!"

So I went up to London to see the head of the A.T.S. to find out if in some way we could provide brides with coupons for wedding-dresses. I was laughed at for even suggesting anything so absurd. Of course the Board of Trade would not release precious coupons for anything so frivolous as a white wedding-gown!

As I sat looking at the severely uniformed and grim powderless faces of the women wearing the insignia of Generals and Brigadiers I was suddenly inspired.

"Wouldn't it be possible," I hazarded, "to get wedding dresses without coupons? What about second-hand ones?"

"You must have a very trusting belief in human nature," someone said acidly, "if you think anyone will part with a wedding-dress without coupons."

I was determined to show they were wrong. I advertised in *The Lady* and bought two really lovely wedding-dresses, one for £7 another for £8. I sent them to the War Office with my compliments and suggested the A.T.S. brides might borrow them for the most important day in their lives and return them afterwards.

The War Office jumped at the idea – if I did the buying – and the W.A.A.F. were not far behind.

Each dress had to be purchased, unpacked, ironed and repacked, but Service women could sweep up the aisle, feeling that for one day at least in their lives they looked and felt like a fairy princess.

Addition: By the end of the War I had bought over a thousand white wedding-gowns and they had all passed through our tiny 400-year-old thatched cottage where we were living in Bedfordshire.

I write a lyric for a song in which I tried to describe what a woman feels who is in love.

> *I dream a secret dream*
> *I search the sky and touch the sea.*
> *I dream of mountains peaking high,*
> *Of forests where no human's been,*
> *And in my dream I search for thee.*
>
> *I dream a secret dream*
> *Of wild delight and love so sweet*
> *That sunshine blinds my quivering eyes*
> *And violets spring beneath my feet,*
> *And in my dreams your lips I meet.*
>
> *I dream a secret dream*
> *I hold a star against my breast,*
> *I dream the moonbeams follow me*
> *In tenderness, in tenderness,*
> *And in my dreams I'm one with thee.*

1944

Great Barford
Bedfordshire

There is a poem which I cut out of a newspaper in 1940 and kept.

I do not remember now which paper it was, so perhaps I may be forgiven for quoting it without permission, for it illustrates so well what I am trying to say about several very young men who lost their lives in the war.

For twenty years you lived and laughed and played
Your glowing youth, and all who knew you laid
Returning tribute at your winged feet
That danced so blithely down the golden street
Where all are good companions ; in the sun
You lived and laughed and played, and found it fun.

I was not with you on your last long flight
Through what tempestuous skies, through what black
*   night,*
But I would wager all that you were gay
And smiling as they pulled the chocks away –
You made your life a party to the end
And even Death must call you now his friend.

1945

London

I have been taken by one of the leaders of the Spiritualist Movement to all the most important Mediums in London. Some of them went into trances, some were 'direct voice' Mediums.

I asked one simple question which helped me decide if they were really in touch with Ronald.

A verse he often quoted to me and in his speeches was written by Robert Browning:

> *The Common Problem, yours, mine, everyone's*
> *Is not to fancy what were fair in life,*
> *Provided it could be, – but, finding first*
> *What may be, then find how to make it fair*
> *Up to our means – a very different thing!*
> *No abstract intellectual plan of Life*
> *Quite irrespective of life's plainest laws,*
> *But one a man, who is a man and nothing more,*
> *May lead within a world which (by your leave)*
> *Is Rome or London – not Fool's Paradise.*

My Biography of him has been a great success, and the Earl of Selborne, with whom when he was Lord Wolmer Ronald worked closely in the House of Commons, asked if he could make a Symposium of Ronald's speeches and beliefs.

Of course I agreed and I have called it 'The Common Problem'.

When the Mediums say: "Ronald is here beside me," I reply: "Will you ask him what he thinks of the Common Problem?"

Not one had the correct answer, and it is inconceivable, remembering Ronald's closeness to me when I wrote his Biography and the way our brains were attuned to each other's, that he would not understand.

Besides this none of them reproduced the strong, vivid positiveness about his conversation which had made him so outstanding in Parliament.

Has nothing survived of his hatred of injustice, his visionary ideas of sweeping reforms, his brilliant, sparkling, inspiring oratory?

I cannot believe that the sender of such dull, drab commonplace messages as these is Ronald.

"What are you doing?" I ask.

"He says he is very busy."

"Doing what?"

"Helping others. He has a desk."

"In what way is he helping people?"

"He says he is very busy."

I remembered almost the same alleged communications from my father after he was killed. If the million men killed in World War I had really been helping those on earth, why had we become embroiled in World War II? It didn't seem as if their efforts had been very successful!

"He says he is often with you."

"Neither my mother or I are aware of it, and we have tried to contact him. Ask him where he has tried to get in touch with us."

"He says in the home."

"In my home or my mother's? And where in the home?"

"He just says in the home."

It is all frustrating, imponderable, inconclusive!

It is idiotic to suppose that as soon as people die they know – if there is survival – all the secrets of the universe. I think they know as little or as much as they knew on earth. But since Ronald had been so brilliant while he was alive, how could these commonplace mutterings be his?

117

This is not to say that Mediums are deliberately trying to deceive those who seek to communicate. They may in all sincerity believe they are in touch with those who are dead. But when people are unhappy and emotionally unbalanced, it is very easy to believe their loved one is present.

1953

Camfield Place
Hatfield

In 1933 we fell in love by the sea in the South of France. We looked into each other's eyes and knew we were meant for each other since the beginning of time.

Everything should have been perfect, but fate, that strange, mysterious power against which there is no appeal, decreed otherwise.

To-day I have written these verses and they bring back so vividly the glory which touched us both for a little while with a love that was part of the Divine.

"SO LONG A TIME"

Is it twenty years since you said good-bye?
I remember your roses made me cry.
And your letter which said so little and yet
I knew it was something I'd never forget.

Twenty years and I can still hear
That note in your voice when our lips were near.
The feel of your arms, your mouth, your hands
Encompass me still like unbreakable bands.

I laugh, seem busy and people say,
"It's wonderful how you are always gay".
But when I think of you I know
Those twenty years have been slow . . . slow . . . slow.

1954

Camfield Place
Hatfield

I have written *The Fascinating Forties* to cheer up women who had reached the age of forty, with the news that there is a great deal of fun in life still to be had! Mentally a person of forty is still on the threshold of greatness.

Women, of course, think most of their beauty, but Diane de Poitiers (whose biography I was to write later) was loved to distraction by Henry II, King of France, nineteen years her junior, until she was sixty.

Ninon de l'Enclos, with her peach-bloom complexion, huge dark eyes and crown of red-gold hair, had lovers until she was over ninety, one of whom shot himself for love of her when she was sixty.

Mary Anne Wyndham married Disraeli when she was forty-seven and gave him thirty-three years of ecstatic happiness. Lady Palmerston was fifty-two when she fell passionately in love with her second husband, and they remained lovers for life.

Far too many women believe that love is a question of having the right waist and bust measurements, or what was later to be called 'vital statistics', and far too many men think, if they are ageing, a young body will make them young again.

Love is something that can mature and become more wonderful, more ecstatic and more perfect as one grows old.

Was it Bernard Shaw who said, 'Youth is too good for the young'?

I think that when we are young we take love, desire and sexual attraction as a matter of course.

But as we grow older we begin to realise how much more enjoyable these things can be when they are savoured and appreciated instead of gobbled up like a hasty meal and forgotten.

1955

Six Mile Bottom
Nr. Newmarket

Today I have visited the site of the lovely historic mansion of Hare Park near Newmarket, where Byron's half-sister lived.

Alas, Hare Park, with its exquisitely proportioned rooms, elegant mantelshelves and delicate staircase, had dry rot and during the war was pulled to the ground.

Only the site remains, looking out over undulating parkland and the fertile plain of Cambridgeshire.

The grass walk with its big stone flower-garlanded urns, where Byron must often have walked and talked, is a wilderness of straying brambles and overgrown branches, and yet there seems to me a certain magic still to be found there.

It is not drear and dead, but alive, and the green of the trees, of grass and shrubs seems to create an illusion of perpetual spring.

Even when the winter lies bleak and dull over the flat country stretching towards Newmarket, the trees stand protective at Hare Park.

The whisper of the wind in their branches seems to create the illusion that something remains of the passions and brilliance, the genius and sinfulness of those who lived and loved there.

Such places are enchanted and they make me ask:

What stirs within my restless heart,
What magic trembles and awakes,
Like ripples from a wind-stirred harp
In this remote enchanted place?

Haunting! taunting, sweet wild singing,
Flash of silver leaping flame
Phantoms mist-blown magic winging
Calling me again . . . again.

How much impression do we make on the places where we live? Who will deny that homes have atmosphere, even as people have personalities?

Perhaps what we call atmosphere is a pot-pourri of personality, character, and emotion accumulated down the centuries, each owner contributing his quota until the house itself becomes a transmitter, vibrating to the life force its secrets.

Can we not understand that a house which has been lived in by a family for many generations becomes part of the family itself?

1955

Malvern
Worcestershire

I am staying with my mother at Malvern. When we are together the conversation invariably turns to Ronald and Tony.

"What do you think they are doing, Mummy?" I ask.

"If only we knew!"

"Both clairvoyants and priests always say that those who have died are busy, that God has work for them to do," I say. "But I want to know what it is. They said the same when Daddy was killed. If he and the million other men who died in World War I were working – to make the world Christian, to stop war – all I can say is that they haven't been very successful!"

"One can only believe that there is a reason, a plan; one can only have faith!" my mother replied.

"That's all right for you, because you have it," I retort. "But I want more. I want a sign. I want to be sure with my logical, materialistic mind that they are alive. Ronald always said he would let us know. If he or Tony came to you, if you saw or heard them, I would believe in their survival. As it is, I am not convinced, I am only groping and longing desperately to know the truth."

My mother sighs; she knows what I am feeling. Despite the fact that her own faith is deep-rooted and unquestionable, she too longs for a sign.

She is absolutely sure that Bertie, Ronald and Tony will all be waiting for her when she dies – that to reach them she has only to pass from this world into the next.

Yet sometimes she must question, as I do, where they are and what they are doing?

She has received a letter from a priest who says:

"May God continue to console and to inspire you. May you catch even a glimpse of His Divine Purpose through the dark cloud of your bereavements. May He let you have a measure of what you so generously give to others; inspiration, conviction that selflessness is pre-eminently worthwhile; and may He bless you – bless you again and again."

My mother places her whole trust in her Church, believing, as she believed when she took the plunge and became a Catholic, that it holds the key to the truth.

But still she is human, she longs to know personally about her husband and her sons, she longs for 'a glimpse of His Divine Purpose'.

A priest who has helped her greatly for many years has told her of a sign he received from his mother who was dead.

It was during the war and he was in North Africa with the 'Desert Rats'. The small company to which he was attached lost their bearings and had to camp for the night.

The Priest lying asleep in the sand with the soldiers, heard his mother's voice which said: "Get up – get up." It was so insistent that he awoke and was absolutely convinced he had heard her.

He got up not only because his mother had told him to do so, but for natural reasons. He was standing alone some little distance away when a shell burst and killed all the men he had been with.

1955

Malvern
Worcestershire

My mother has told me what happened to her last night. She is now seventy-eight and has suffered so greatly in her life. Her husband whom she adored was killed in 1918, her two sons Ronald and Tony, to whom she dedicated her life were killed at Dunkirk.

She had become a Catholic just before the war and her faith and courage sustained her, so that when she heard of her sons' deaths she said:

"If crying would bring them back I would cry my eyes out, but as it is I must go on trying to help other people."

At the beginning of April she went as usual to Mass in the Catholic church at Malvern. It was eight o'clock on Thursday morning. It was a cold day with a promise of rain in the grey sky. The Church seemed dark save for the candles flickering on the altar.

As my mother entered, she saw there was a coffin in the chancel. There were no flowers and she saw to her surprise, there were also no mourners or strangers in the church, only two women whom she knew well and who were always present every Thursday.

She spoke to both of them and asked who was dead.

"A poor Pole," was the answer.

"Hasn't he any relatives here?" my mother enquired.

"No one – it does seem sad!"

My mother's heart was touched.

"Let us offer our intentions for him," she suggested. The two women agreed and my mother knelt down.

For the first time for years she didn't pray for her

own family – she concentrated her thoughts, her prayers, her whole self on the poor, forgotten man who was passing from this world without anyone to wish him Godspeed.

The service began, the Church was very quiet save for the priest's voice. There was hardly any light coming from the east window, for it had begun to rain outside, and the flames of the candles were golden against the gloom.

My mother prayed, whispering the lovely prayers that the Church has for centuries used for the dead. She added her own – prayers that came from a heart that had always responded to whatever had been asked of it.

The sanctuary bell tinkled and she raised her head, preparatory to rising.

A brilliant white light came from above to envelop the altar. It was like no light she had ever seen before – it was blinding, beautiful and so vivid that it hurt her eyes to look at it.

For a moment she stared at it spell-bound, then she approached and knelt to receive the Sacrament. The light was still there, although she bent her head humbly and was no longer looking directly at it.

She received the Body of Christ; then, as the priest placed the Host in the Tabernacle, the light vanished. There were only the candles, the general dimness and the flowerless, unattended coffin. For a moment my mother could only think:

"The poor man has passed over peacefully; my prayers have been heard."

Then, as she knelt again in her own pew, she realised that it was so much more. It was the sign that I also had sought, the glimpse of God's Divine Purpose that she had longed to receive.

A reassurance that Bertie, Ronald and Tony would be waiting for her when she died – a promise not only of their survival, but also that their love for her was not just for their lifetime but for all eternity!

1956

Camfield Place
Hatfield

I have discovered a great deal about old people this year. One true story which I told in a newspaper has brought me, I am glad to say, hundreds of letters asking if there was any way the ordinary public could help.

It was the story of an old woman who lived alone in South London. One day she was discovered dead in her bed. She had been dead for over a week.

There was a diary by her side, and day after day, week after week, there was the same simple entry – '*Nobody came*'.

I write this poem which has been read on Radio Luxemburg.

> *An old woman lay in her narrow bed;*
> *Every day it was just the same.*
> *She hoped for a chat, a laugh, a game,*
> *But as daylight ended all she said was*
> *"Nobody came! Nobody came!"*
>
> *Outside people hurried – the sun was bright,*
> *But all she knew was the endless pain.*
> *She waited and watched for fading light,*
> *And as the day ended she murmured again*
> *"Nobody came! Nobody came!"*

1957

The Delawarr Laboratories
Oxford

I am deeply interested in the Black Box which is the subject of much controversy, and I am visiting the Headquarters of its inventor, George de la Warr.

It would be impossible not to be impressed by his deep sincerity and his strong personality. When I arrive the garden surrounding his Laboratory is filled with flowers. They seem to me to glow with unusually vivid colours.

There is also an impression of light and peace. It is difficult to explain in words, but there was something supernormal about the surroundings which I both saw and felt.

George is convinced that pre-physical energy is vital to our existence and for years he had been experimenting with Laboratory instruments to link the ethereal or astral plane with the physical.

His diagnostic instrument has become known as the Black Box because it is covered in black leather. It looks like an electric machine, but it is in fact a carefully worked out extension of the operator's psychic faculty and is 'powered' with mind and thought.

George shows me a photograph of a knife which had been 'thought' onto a Radionic camera without a film. And I see a number of the celebrated Boxes at work.

A drop of the patient's blood enables him to be healed through the power engendered in the Box through the operator.

A great friend of mine had for years suffered with an acute pain in her back. A number of doctors had said there was nothing they could do and she must live with it.

One morning she woke up and said to her husband:

"I can't believe it but incredibly after all this time the pain has gone!"

It was only some days later when she was still without pain that her mother-in-law confessed that without telling anyone she had sent one of her letters to 'The Box'.

The only thing that worries me here at Oxford is that George de la Warr has so many patients that he has to have extra helpers to operate the Boxes.

George and his charming wife Marjorie are both extremely psychic and remarkably intuitive. I am convinced that they can help and heal suffering, but I am slightly sceptical as to whether other people have such gifted vibrations.

There is however no doubt in my mind that here in this lovely quiet laboratory there is the force and power of esoteric thought.

Addition: In 1960 a case of fraud was brought against George de la Warr. In the ensuing High Court action for damages, he was openly backed by a section of the Medical profession and each and every allegation of fraud was dismissed by the Judge.

A remarkable array of witnesses for defence included qualified doctors, who had used The Box themselves, scientists, physicists and veterinary surgeons.

George de la Warr who died when he was 64 will, I believe, rank as one of the pioneers of the 20th Century in his attempts to lead mankind towards an ultimate awareness.

1957

Camfield Place
Hatfield

When I came to Camfield, I had the house blessed in case there might be a ghost in it. After my experiences in Somerset I disliked ghosts.

But what is extraordinary is that now we have the ghost of one of our dogs who had been 'put to sleep'.

My maid, who has always been psychic, has seen the dog two or three times in the hall, and I have seen it twice.

Once it was lying under the table, and because I was carrying a big vase of flowers I pushed it with my foot saying: "Do get out of the way!" thinking it was Murray – one of the other spaniels. I touched nothing!

At one time the ghost dog was so fierce that whenever Murray tried to eat his dinner in the dining-room he would give a shriek as if he had been bitten, and then back away from his dish snarling as if another dog was trying to take it from him.

We have grown quite used to the ghost. It doesn't worry us, it was one of our own dogs, and it has all been written up in *The Stately Ghosts of England*. Tom Corbet, the Irish clairvoyant, came down and talked to me about it.

He had been to Longleat, Littlecote, Salisbury Hall, an innumerable other Stately Homes where there were all sorts of remarkable ghosts with heads under arms, and he was obviously not very impressed with my poor little dog ghost. But when he left he said to me:

"Have you got a son?"

"Yes," I replied.

"Does he drive a car?"

I nodded, and Tom Corbet said: "Tell him to be very careful for the next two or three days."

It was really rather a wicked thing to say and I was terrified because my son, Glen, was on the Continent motoring with his cousin.

I managed to reach him by telephone in Brussels.

"Please, darling, be careful," I pleaded.

"Don't fuss, Mummy!"

It was the reply of sons to anxious mothers all through the ages.

The next night I was awoken about three o'clock in the morning by the noise of police cars beneath my bedroom window. I put my head out and asked what was happening.

"There has been an accident to one of Mr. McCorquodale's cars," I was told.

What had really happened was that a young man-servant returning from a night-out after drinking a lot with some friends, missed his way when the road curved and drove straight into a ditch.

He turned the car over, missing a telegraph-post by inches, and although he had only a few scratches the car was a total wreck.

1959

New Delhi
India

My son Ian and I are in India. It is the most exciting journey I have ever made. To-day we lunched with the Prime Minister, Pundit Nehru. He arrived from Congress where he had delivered a long speech. He was tired and I thought tense.

He is a great man, holding together one of the most populous countries in the world by sheer personality.

Gandhi preached and lived non-violence. Nehru has only his astute brain, his deep love of India, and the facility for walking a tight-rope with which to keep Communism from crossing the border.

We were only six to lunch so we could talk intimately. That morning in Congress Pundit Nehru had said, "I hope we shall avoid saying things which add to the already large amount of bitterness and ill-will in the world."

To him the past is past.

"You were imprisoned for fourteen years of your life," a friend of mine said to him. "You were beaten and misused. Don't you hate the British who did this to you?"

Nehru shook his head.

"Does it matter tomorrow?" he asks.

When he speaks of India, I feel the love he has for his country rising like a tidal wave within him.

It is a tempestuous, fighting force, so strong, so overpowering that one thinks of him as tall, physically as well as mentally. He is in fact only 5 feet 5 inches in height.

He also has a spiritual awareness, strictly kept under

control because it could carry him away from the hurly-burly of every-day politics.

Yet when we say goodbye and, with the inevitable courteous politeness of India, he takes us to our car, I feel the power vibrating within him.

He can link the Life Force to his own needs, he can use himself as a transmitter. On this rests the peace and the prosperity of 600,000,000 people.

1959

Agra
India

India is extremely conducive to clairvoyance and religious manifestations.

It is not by chance that Indians are the most religious people in the world, and everywhere one sees Holy men shaken and consumed by the power of their faith.

There is something in India which stirs one's inner self and because of it strange things happen.

Ian and I had motored from Jaipur to Agra. It was a long way and it was very, very hot. When we arrived at the hotel late this afternoon, I was shown into a charming newly decorated bedroom.

Just as I was about to say that it suited me very well, I realised that there was no air-conditioning.

"I must have a bedroom with air-conditioning," I told the proprietor.

He was not an Indian, who would have been charming, but a rather disagreeable German. We started the usual boring argument.

The rooms had been booked months ahead, air conditioning had been asked for and promised – all the usual palaver, which is so exhausting when one is tired.

At last, somewhat reluctantly, the proprietor said there were rooms outside the main hotel looking onto an unkempt garden at the back. We went to see them.

They seemed quite adequate, but they certainly needed redecorating. The mosquito nets were old and tattered. There was, however, air-conditioning and I felt that was all that mattered.

We started to unpack and then suddenly over some

quite trivial thing I started to have a scene with Ian. I raged. I screamed at him and kept reiterating, "I want to go home! I won't stay here any longer, I must go home!"

Even while I spoke I knew that I was not myself, but someone called Annie, who was married to a British soldier at the beginning of the century when they had white veils hanging behind their topees to protect their necks. I can still see her quite clearly.

She came from Glasgow in Scotland; she hated India, she was desperately homesick, terribly unhappy and she wanted to go home. I understood, too, in some manner that I can't explain, that Annie was dead and that she was buried somewhere in the country she hated.

I am certain that people's emotions, passions – violent actions – imprint themselves on the atmosphere. That may be why people are so often afraid and restless in houses where dramatic events have taken place.

1959

Benares
India

We have flown to Benares, the Holy City, which means more to the Indians than any place on earth. There are thousands of pilgrims from all over India bathing in the Ganges, swarming down the steps towards the river and sleeping on the banks at night, wherever they could find a place to lie.

It is an amazing sight and even more amazing to walk among them. For they are all lost in a little world of their own; immersed in their own prayers, they hardly seem to notice what goes on around them.

Yesterday we hired a boat and went up the Ganges in the very early morning as the dawn broke. We went again at night, and each time it had a charm and a mystery that is not easy to communicate.

There was so much faith pouring into one small place, one felt the air ought to be blue from the vibrations of those who believed so fervently that they would be blessed because they had bathed.

In the hotel I was told that an Englishwoman wanted to meet me. My heart sank, but though I particularly didn't want to meet the English there was nothing I could do about it. How thankful I am now I didn't refuse.

Miss Violet Sydney was eighty years old and looked rather like an old tortoise. I found she had been a close associate of Madame Alexandra David-Neel, the only woman Lama in the world.

Miss Sydney told us how, when she told Madame Alexandra David-Neel that she was living in Benares, the Frenchwoman had said to her:

"And have you seen the burning ghats?"

"I have seen them from a boat," Miss Sydney replied.

"You are a coward," was the accusation.

"I wasn't going to have anyone calling an English-woman a coward," Miss Sydney told me. "I went down into the ghats and watched eight bodies burned. The poor ones cannot afford very much wood, so they have to be turned over and over like a chicken on a spit.

"It was a strange, rather horrible experience. One doesn't realise until one is there that the knee-bones turn translucent in the fire, or that every corpse reacts differently to the flames."

I asked Miss Sydney about Madame David-Neel's extraordinary experience which she relates in *With Mystics and Magicians in Tibet*. She had invented a character and thought of him so often and so clearly that he became a living entity.

He even assumed a personality of his own, until she could not be rid of him, and he became malicious and difficult. What was more, he was even seen by other people.

"Did you see him?" I asked.

Miss Sydney shook her head.

"He had gone by the time I met Madame David-Neel," she said. "She had dissolved him though it had been a tremendous effort for her. But I know other people who did see him."

"What have been your experiences?" I asked.

She smiled.

"No-one who has experienced anything really mystical is allowed to tell," she answered. "No Yogi will take money for anything he does, and any real Yogi who speaks of his powers will lose them. Always remember that, or you will be deceived and tricked."

1959

Khatmandu
Nepal

To-day we met the members of the British Sola Khumba Expedition who were off to climb the Ame Dablan.

This mountain of 25,494 feet has never been climbed and has defied a number of attempts. But six Englishmen and one English woman hope to conquer it within the next few weeks.

Ian and I talked to them and found they were very diverse types – one had been at Magdalene College, Cambridge where Ian had been, another was a clerk from Wolverhampton, the Doctor from Newcastle.

They all belonged to the same climbing Club and were fired with enthusiasm and a determination to reach the top.

The Nepalese shook their heads. The British were doing this climb in a very economical way with only seventy porters for the seven of them.

The Italians, we were told, had taken seven hundred porters for a similar expedition last year.

The leader was however, quite convinced that any more porters were unnecessary.

"Polythene," he told me, "has replaced the old-fashioned way of keeping things water-tight. It lightens the load of each porter by several pounds."

The sun was shining, the garden where they gathered was brilliant with flowers, the sky was clear and blue; only the mountains were shrouded with mist.

I had a sense of danger. I knew indisputably that one, if not more, of these bright-faced eager young men would not return.

Ame Dablan would preserve her inviolability and the gods who lived on the heights would revenge themselves on those who trespassed on their territory.

"Don't go!" I longed to say. I wanted to plead with them to change their minds.

But who would have listened? They would merely have thought me an hysterical woman.

Addition: We learnt when we returned home that two of the young men were killed and the Expedition did not reach the top.

1959

Khatmandu
Nepal

We have flown from India to Nepal and to-day in
Khatmandu I visited the Living Goddess.

A child of six is chosen for this position for which there
is strong competition. She is then invested as the Goddess of Destruction to destroy the King's enemies and all
that threatens him.

She remains a Goddess until she reaches puberty.
She is not allowed out, except on ceremonial occasions,
and is kept in a house with her family, although she
has a courtyard to play in.

We were allowed to call on her and, standing in a
courtyard deep with pigeon-droppings, to speak to her
when she appeared at a third floor window.

She is now about nine and is heavily made up with
great slanting lines drawn from the corner of her eyes up
to her temples. She has flowers upon her head.

She glances at us sulkily for some time and the guide
tells us in a hoarse whisper that if she was unhappy everyone believes that a great calamity would befall the King.

Then she says something to her mother who repeats it
to the guide. He translates it to us.

"She admires the lady's hat very much."

I am wearing a hat made of white flowers with green
leaves. The Living Goddess and her mother can talk of
nothing else. I manage to extort the information that
there were four brothers and three sisters, but all they
really want to talk about is my hat!

1959

In the Foothills of the Himalayas

We were motoring along the lovely roads of the foothills when I saw six Holy men with their gold tipped staffs.

"Where are they going?" I asked.

"They have been to see a Holy Man who is very respected round here," I was told.

With great difficulty I persuaded our guide to ask if the Holy Man would see us.

We found him in a lovely wood surrounded by a barbed iron fence, beside his chair was a potty which seemed somewhat unnecessary.

He is cared for by two families who have become his disciples and are obviously very devoted to him. They approach him with awe and respect.

Sivapuri Baba is one hundred and thirty-two years old. He was born in 1826 in South India and has gone all round the world, staying in England for five years until 1901. He speaks perfect English and is, I am told, a great philosopher.

He is extremely interesting to talk to. He is not deaf, he has his own teeth, a long beard and, although he is a little bald on top of his head, he has quite a lot of hair.

"I am getting frail now," he told me with a smile, and his eyes shone like a young boy's with mischief and amusement and a kind of wisdom which one could not explain.

He spoke of self-discipline, of avoiding violence and anger and lust. And then I said to him:

"Won't you tell me some of your own spiritual experiences?"

"If I eat a delicious fruit," he said, "I know what the taste is. But there are no words in which I can describe it to you. To know what it is like you must taste it for yourself."

It was India which gave me so much and opened new vistas I had never known before. I tried to paint a picture of that entrancing country in verse:

"INDIA"

Heaped fruit, vegetables and grain,
Mustard, masala, musk and ghee.
Dust rising in clouds to fall again
On silk and silver, gold and tea.
Crowds drifting, jostling, wandering where?
With Brahmini bulls, sacred and old.
Veiled women giggling stop and stare,
Or listen to the storyteller's ode.
This is India under a burning sun,
The glory of the dawn o'er plain and peak.
Swift opal twilight when the day is done.
And nights of whispered magic as men speak
Of gods and love, rebellion, battles won.
Here hides the truth for which I seek.

1959

Khatmandu
Nepal

We learn that the world is excited by the news of the Dalai Lama's flight from Lhasa.

"There are 25,000 refugees on the borders of Nepal and Tibet," we were told. The papers also said that there were fears for the Dalai Lama's safety, and that he may have been captured.

We went to-day to Bodhanath to see a two-thousand-five-hundred-year-old Buddhist temple. One of the holiest places in the world, according to the Buddhists, it is very large and white and surmounted by a high square tower on each side of which are painted two huge, vividly coloured eyes.

We went a little way down the road where there was another temple. This belonged to ten Mongolian lamas who had fled from Tibet a few years earlier because they were afraid of coming under Chinese domination. They were of the sect dedicated to poverty and celibacy.

The temple has been painted by hand in the most glowing and beautiful colours. The gold and silver work could only have been achieved with loving care and had, indeed, been done by the lamas themselves and by travelling pilgrims who had stayed for a week or so and made this contribution in payment of hospitality.

The monks prepared us a cup of Tibetan tea. It is made of tea which has been pressed into blocks, with butter, salt and bean flour. It is the main sustenance of every traveller in Tibet, and was what the Dalai Lama himself existed on during his flight.

"Have you news of the Dalai Lama?" I ask.

The Lamas shook their heads, but they were smiling, and Ian said to them:

"Is he safe?"

They nodded.

"How do you know that?" we asked.

They explained through the guide that they didn't know; they had had no news; there had been no message from Tibet, no-one had been able to get through for months.

"But you know he is safe?" we persisted.

They nodded, all smiles, and one of the younger ones laughed gaily for no apparent reason. Still laughing, they ran outside to show us the six foot long ceremonial trumpets which are blown from the monastery on very special occasions. And then, because something was making them happy, they blew them for us.

Addition: It was nearly a week afterwards that the world learned that the Dalai Lama was safe and had reached India despite the Chinese efforts to capture him.

1959

Camfield Place
Hatfield

My mother was first told in June that she has a stone in her kidneys. The doctor has said it is impossible to dissolve it and she will have to have an operation.

I am very worried as we have found in the past that she cannot take an anaesthetic and she is now eighty-two.

She is staying with me and I ask her if she is in pain and she admits she is. Suddenly I give a cry:

"I'm mad not to have thought of it before, Mummy! I will telephone Mrs. Gibson at once."

Mrs. Gibson is a healer, a marvellous Scottish woman whom I first met through a friend who is very musical. She had a friend whom I also knew, who is a very famous prima donna, described as 'a pocket Venus' who seems too tiny for her magnificent voice.

She has one precious son of six who suddenly was taken ill and after many X-rays she was told he had cancer and must have an artificial rectum. As this operation is very seldom really successful she was distraught.

She was making a special appearance in Glasgow and the night before the operation she rushed off the stage after her performance to change and take the night express to London.

As she was changing a Mrs. Gibson whom she knew as a fan, came to her dressing-room. The prima donna said:

"I can't stop now, my son is having an operation to-morrow morning."

Mrs. Gibson asked her what was wrong with him and was answered rather perfunctorily as the prima donna rushed away to catch her train.

She reached London and went to the Hospital. She was desperately afraid of what was happening in the operating room.

The surgeon came out to say:

"Everything is all right, we found nothing wrong."

"What do you mean, nothing wrong?" the mother asked.

"What I say."

"Are you telling me that you have cut up my poor little boy and caused me all this terrible anxiety unnecessarily?"

"You do not understand," the surgeon answered, "this is a miracle. The X-ray showed very clearly what was wrong, but when we operated we found nothing."

Dazed, the prima donna went back to Glasgow. After her next performance Mrs. Gibson came round to her dressing-room. She looked very tired.

"It was all right," she smiled.

"It was, but how did you know?"

"I and my circle of Absent Healers have been on our knees all night," was the reply.

I telephoned Mrs. Gibson a dedicated woman, who would take nothing for her work of healing, and told her about my mother.

"Don't worry," she said in her broad Scottish accent. "Your mother will be all right."

Addition: My mother has telephoned me to say her doctor suggested one more X-ray before she went into hospital, so that she would be the shortest time possible under an anaesthetic.

"Darling it is unbelievable!" my mother cried. "The stone has gone! The doctor says it is a miracle!"

1960

Camfield Place
Hatfield

No doctor or psychologist really understands the working of the human mind. An idea planted in the subconscious may take years to materialise, and no-one can explain why some people have a sixth sense.

I believe this sixth sense is the instinct we used before 'civilisation' battered it out of us, by laughing at and deriding anything we could not actually prove mathematically, see or touch.

Twelve hours before the Agadir earthquake a Moroccan woman packed her few possessions and begged her husband to take her and their children into the countryside. Her sense of impending catastrophe was so strong that some of the neighbours followed her.

The houses in which they lived were crushed in the earthquake by a neighbouring modern building. Those who remained were all killed.

Last year on the very day harvesting started, one of our farm workmen who had been with us for nine years gave a week's notice. He told us his wife wanted him to go into a factory, and he had heard of an opening. I was annoyed and told him so.

"Any other time wouldn't matter," I said, "but harvest is a crucial time for every farmer. It's almost impossible to replace you at such short notice and that makes it very hard on the other men."

He was adamant, and without thinking why I said it, and indeed rather surprised at myself, I added:

"This new job won't bring you anything but bad luck, I know that."

A few months ago I was horrified to hear that the man had been killed by a bus as he was cycling to work!

1962

London

Peter Howard, who had been a Lobby correspondent in the House of Commons when Ronald was a Member of Parliament, became head of the Oxford Group Movement after Frank Buchmann's death in 1961.

He asks me to dine at their headquarters in Berkeley Square. There is a large gathering of guests including several adherents in Japanese costume.

Dame Flora MacLeod, the 28th Chief of the MacLeod, is piped into dinner by her own piper. It is her 85th birthday and she carries herself magnificently.

No alcohol is served, but a fruit-juice cocktail is delicious and so is the dinner, served by those who have dedicated themselves to the Movement and give up their holidays to cook and wait.

The house is magnificently furnished with antiques and it seems strange to think of pacifists in a house which once belonged to the brilliant, if aggressive, Clive of India, who as one of the creators of British power in India was described as 'a heaven-born General'.

Not long after we dined Peter Howard died. When he was dead I was suddenly aware of a play that he wanted me to write.

It was there in my mind every act, every word, every movement, complete. The Group have their own theatre which I had visited, and I know I only had to set down what Peter was telling me and it would be performed.

But something stopped me. I was not actually in unison with the Movement. I had not been particularly impressed with Frank Buchmann as a spiritual leader. I was definitely against pacifism.

Yet I still feel guilty that I did not do what Peter wanted. I still question if I was right or wrong to refuse.

1962

Camfield Place
Hatfield

I am sixty and every day I shall try to say this prayer which has been given to me by the Church of Our Lady of Mount Carmel:

"Lord, Thou knowest better than I know myself that I am growing older, and will some day be old. Keep me from the fatal habit of thinking that I must say something on every subject and on every occasion. Release me from craving to straighten out everybody's affairs.

"Make me thoughtful but not moody, helpful, but not bossy. With my vast store of wisdom, it seems a pity not to use it all – but, Thou knowest, Lord, that I want a few friends at the end.

"Keep my mind free from the recital of endless details . . . give me wings to get to the point. Seal my lips on aches and pains. They are increasing and love of rehearsing them is becoming sweeter as the years go by. I dare not ask for grace enough to enjoy the tales of others' pains, but help me to endure them with patience.

"I do not ask for improved memory, but for growing humility and a lessening cock-sureness when my memory seems to clash with the memories of others. Teach me the glorious lesson that occasionally I may be mistaken.

"Keep me reasonably sweet; I do want to be a saint . . . but not one who is hard to live with . . . for a sour old person is one of the crowning works of the devil.

"Give me the ability to see good things in unexpected places and talents in unexpected people, and please give me the grace to tell them so."

How little we appreciate our youth, how profligate we are with the years as they fly by. Only as we grow older do we cherish every hour, every minute of each day because the sands are running out.

"YOUTH"

The world was unknown, a mysterious place,
An adventure to move, to breathe in the sun.
To get to the top was only a race
Anyone could run.

That was youth, when everything was new,
Full of ideals and faith a vivid flame.
Unspoilt, untired and courageous too,
Living a game.

Slowly the idols fall, bitter to know,
That friends no longer friendly, envy, defame,
Tired of the battle, getting old and slow
Until we rise again.

1963

Camfield Place
Hatfield

It is extremely difficult to decide if numerology is coincidence, superstition or fact. Lucky charms are the same. Can anyone sensible really believe in them? And yet many strange and inexplicable things happen.

In 1914 my father, taking his Company into the front line trenches in Flanders, lost his swagger stick (carried by every British Officer). He pulled a thick, rough piece of wood out of a hedge and carried that instead.

He lost none of his men in that engagement, and after a few weeks the Company began to believe the stick brought them luck.

My father drilled a hole through the wood and it was attached to his waist by a bootlace. He used it for four years. His men refused to go into the front line without it.

In 1918 he came home on leave and left it with my mother to have three silver bands put round it, commemorating the great battles in which it had taken part. He went back to France without it and was killed a few weeks later.

No-one can resist the idea of 'buying' good luck. In the window of a scruffy little junk-shop in Portsmouth my mother saw a china vase she thought I might like, but on closer inspection it turned out to be cracked. She looked round.

"What is that?" she asked, seeing on a high shelf at the back of the shop a Chinese figure of Hotei, the big-bellied God of Happiness.

"Oh, I don't want to sell that," the shopkeeper

replied. "People round here think it's lucky, they hire it from me for a week or a few days at a time."

Of course my mother had to buy it after that.

"Put it in a place of honour," the shopkeeper said. "And treat him with great respect."

I had the figure in my bedroom until the war came. Then, when we left our house in London, Hotei was bundled into a shoe box. After that everything seemed to go wrong. Big things and little things, everything in my life seemed disastrous.

I remembered a superstition that putting something unlucky into the soil or under water destroyed its power. I took the God of Happiness and drove with him into Hyde Park.

I stopped on the bridge over the Serpentine and dropped him into the water. He made a faint splash. I felt as if I was disposing of 'the body', but at the same time it was as if a weight had fallen from my shoulders!

1964

Camfield Place
Hatfield

My beloved husband, Hugh, died suddenly on December 29th, 1963, one day after we had celebrated twenty-seven years of great happiness.

He was a quiet person who hated publicity, and having loved me for eight years before we were married he was the most contented man I have ever known.

Once I said to him: "If a fairy could wave a magic wand and give you anything you wanted, what would you wish to have?"

Hugh thought for a moment and replied: "I have everything I have ever wanted."

He loved me deeply but he believed that death was the end of everything; there was no after-life, no meeting in another world with those we loved.

After his death I had a message which told me he had been mistaken. I have written down exactly what happened so that it will help other people.

On July 31st, 1917, at the Third Battle of Ypres, 2nd Lieut. Hugh McCorquodale received the Military Cross – "for his gallantry and devotion to duty during the action. It was largely due to his fine personal example and skilful handling of his Company that the enemy counter-attack was delayed."

My husband was just nineteen years old when he was posted to the 6th Battalion in Flanders. Two months later came the terrible slaughter at Passchendaele.

In this battle the expectation of a subaltern's life was twenty minutes. On July 31st there were 279 casualties in

156

the Battalion, and Hugh was severely – almost mortally – wounded.

In attacking the enemy trenches he was hit with a sniper's dum-dum bullet which passed right through his right shoulder and out of his back exploding as it went. This among other injuries, collapsed his lung and smashed three ribs. He turned head over heels and lay out in No-Man's-Land for forty-eight hours.

"You were very near to death," I said to him when we married. "Did you see angels, hear voices, or even feel you were being helped or sustained?"

"No," he replied. "I just felt very tired and far away from all the noise of the battle."

During the second night Hugh was carried in on a man's back and received a number of shrapnel wounds in the process. At the Field Dressing Station they treated only the shrapnel wounds, not realising he was injured elsewhere.

He was carried down to the Base, but the shelling was so bad that the stretcher-bearers dropped him continually, and when he eventually arrived at No. 9 Red Cross Hospital at Calais he was so covered in mud they did not realise he was an officer and he was at first put in the Tommies' ward.

When the doctors examined Hugh they said there was nothing they could do and there wasn't a chance of his survival. He was therefore, as was the practice in those days, put outside in a tent in the grounds of the hospital by himself to die.

On August 25th, his uncle, General Lord Horne (of Stirkoke), who was commanding the First Army, was informed and he sent for Hugh's parents to come over from England to say 'Good-bye' to their son. Mr. and Mrs. Harold McCorquodale crossed the Channel and saw Hugh for what they thought was the last time.

Hugh had fortunately been taken to a 'rich' hospital which was run by the Canadians, and they gave him port and champagne when they dressed his wounds and the rest of the time he was under heroin.

157

He lay for four weeks without food, in a state of semi-consciousness, and we now know that leaving him alone and letting him get over the shock was what saved his life.

After attending five hospitals and having innumerable operations, Hugh survived.

He was a 'show piece' for the doctors, as they considered it a tremendous achievement that they had kept him alive, and he remembered being constantly 'shown off' to visiting Specialists.

When he was discharged the doctors said to him:

"It is a miracle you are alive. Nothing more can be done by surgery, so never let anyone fiddle about with you. You must trust to nature and live with your disability." ·

It was advice he was to stick to all his life and gave him what amounted to almost a fear of doctors.

Hugh was listed as 40% disabled and received a pension which at the time of his death, was £185. 16s. 0d. a year!

His convalescence was very slow and when I met him first in 1927 I was told by various members of his family, including his mother, that he wasn't expected to live long and if he ever got influenza he would die.

We often talked about 'the after life' especially when Ronald and Tony were both killed at Dunkirk.

"Do you really believe," I would say to my husband, "that all Ronald's struggle to help other people is wasted? The times he went hungry so that he could buy books on politics? The years he spent in the Research Department of the Conservative Central Office? The difficulties of money, of working until he made himself ill because he couldn't afford a secretary? Has all that hope, ambition, energy, and faith died with him?"

"I'm afraid so," my husband would answer.

He was a very quiet, gentle man, who never forced his opinions on anyone, but if I asked him what he thought, he always told me the truth.

On December 29th, 1963, after two days of slight

bronchitis Hugh got out of bed and collapsed. The scar tissues from the terrible wounds he had received in 1917 had touched his heart.

The day before, though the doctor said there was no need for anxiety, I was instinctively alarmed and I rang Mrs. Gibson. I told her about Hugh and she promised to ring me back.

When she did so she said:

"I must be honest, dear, and tell you there is nothing I can do; his time has come. I have covered him in blue and he will pass peacefully."

I did not believe her and slammed down the telephone.

I had always known Hugh's life hung on a thread and I was deeply grateful for having had him with me for so long.

He did not suffer and for him it was the peaceful, quick death he would have wanted. But that did not assuage the ghastly shock and the terrible sense of loss.

I had never seen anyone dead before – all my family had died in France. As I stood beside him as he lay in a blue bed wearing blue pyjamas, I could not believe when he had loved me so much that he had left me alone.

A week after the funeral my maid, who had been with me for over twenty-five years said:

"Have you noticed the wonderful scent of carnations outside Mr. McCorquodale's dressing room?"

"No," I replied. "Are you sure? There haven't been any carnations in the house since the funeral and those in the wreaths had no fragrance, not in December."

"I was so surprised at the strength of the perfume," my maid went on, "that I called the daily woman and drew her attention to it. She smelt it too but said it must be something someone had put in their bath."

I didn't think any more about this conversation, but the next morning I got up at 8 o'clock as usual to give my son Glen his breakfast before leaving for London. There is an entresol with only a skylight outside my bedroom, on to which opened the doors from my husband's dressing room, his bathroom and the room in which he died.

As I crossed the entresol I was suddenly aware of the marvellous, almost overpowering scent of carnations. It was unlike any carnations I had ever smelt in England – it was the true exotic fragrance of Malmaisons which I hadn't known for years.

I stood for a moment feeling astounded, then had to hurry downstairs in case Glen missed his train. When he had gone, I came upstairs and the scent was still there but fainter.

I thought I must have imagined it but the following morning it was there again. It was I discovered in patches, the strongest scent being next to my husband's dressing room. Some mornings it wasn't there at all, or I couldn't smell it until I returned upstairs after breakfast.

The fragrance came and went for three weeks. I asked a friend of mine who had been a Medium if she noticed anything not saying what I was thinking.

She identified the unmistakable scent of Malmaison Carnations and found it all round my bedroom door.

I then knew exactly why it was there. My husband and I had always bought red carnations when we went abroad. Every year we went to Paris for a 'second honeymoon'. The first thing we would do on arrival was to drive to the Madeleine. Outside there are always rows of colourful flower stalls.

Hugh would buy me a huge bunch of red carnations before we went into the Church and said a prayer for our marriage. This was something we had done on our first honeymoon and repeated every year except during the war.

The carnations would be arranged in my bedroom.

Each evening when we went out to dinner Hugh would wear one in his buttonhole.

If anything was a symbol of our happiness and our closeness to each other, it was red carnations. Now I understand why the scent of them was near my door. It could only mean one thing, that Hugh was trying to tell me he had been wrong.

He had found a way to convey to me the truth – there is an after-life, there is survival after death.

1963

Camfield Place
Hatfield

"GYPSIES"

Hustled, insulted, moved from place to place
The gypsies are an alien race
But no one cares.

How to find work with open mouths to feed?
How can their children learn to write or read?
But no one cares.

Dark eyes, dark skinned the gypsies roam
Persecuted, cursed, no where is home.
But no one cares.

Addition: I cared and the story of how I changed the
Law of Great Britain follows.

1964

Camfield Place
Hatfield

I had after Ronald's death felt that in a small way, I must carry his idea of service to others. That was why I became a County Councillor for Hertfordshire in 1955.

Ronald had always hated and fought against injustice, which was why I knew he was inspiring and guiding me when I came across a flagrant and incredible injustice of the Law.

What happened was this – our local District-Nurse came one morning to give me an injection. While she was giving it she said:

"What happens about the education of gypsy children? Can they go to school?"

I enquired why she asked the question.

"There is a gypsy family near here," she said. "One of the women is having a baby and has to keep near St. Albans City Hospital as she is to go there when it is due. The whole family, there are three caravans of them, are kept on the move and fined whenever they stop. In one of the other caravans there is a little girl of eight and she is very anxious to attend school, but it doesn't seem possible as they must keep moving."

"I'm afraid I don't know the answer," I said, "but I am going to County Hall to the Education Committee this afternoon, and I'll ask."

Accordingly I rose in the Education Committee and said to the Chairman:

"What is done about the schooling of gypsy children? I know there are quite a number of them in this county."

The Chairman looked at the Director of Education

and said in an aside: "That's a hard one!" So I knew that actually nothing was being done.

I decided to see for myself and I took with me a reporter on the *Herts Advertiser*, our county newspaper.

We went to Colney Heath, which had been one of the traditional gypsy camping-places since the time of Henry VIII when the gypsies first arrived in England.

It was a warm sunny day, and although few people will believe it the occupants of the first caravan I came to were sitting outside on the grass listening to the schools broadcast.

I had also taken with me a gypsy missionary. He was a Romany and known as Gypsy Williams. He introduced me, after explaining that I was not connected with the police, to an elderly gypsy woman called Leanda Davis, who had the high cheekbones, the dark flashing eyes and the hair falling in ringlets of the traditional Romany.

She was the mother of ten children and already had innumerable grandchildren.

"Our children want to learn to read and write," she said. "We realise to-day that they have got to make their way in a modern world, and without schooling how will they manage?"

I met her grandchild Linda, the girl of eight whom the District Nurse had told me about. She was an extremely pretty child, bright and intelligent, and she told me quite positively she would like to go to school.

I then talked with some of the other gypsies; there were nearly thirty caravans of them at Colney Heath.

"Have any of the children been to school?" I asked.

There was a great deal of palaver among the 'didicoys' who are the half-caste gypsies. Finally a boy of seventeen, who was rather shy, told me that he had been to school and could write his name.

"I can't do sums or read," he confessed, "I wish I could."

"Did you like school?" I enquired.

He nodded.

"I loved the games," he said, and his face lit up.

163

"How long were you at school?" I asked.

"A month!" he replied.

I remembered that at Camfield I had a book written in 1816 by a man who had made a survey of the gypsies all over England. In it he referred to the gypsies in Hertfordshire and said there were sixty families of them. He added:

"It is disgraceful in this year and age that nothing is being done about their education!"

I went back to the Davis family. They told me they had all been born in Hertfordshire on the exact spot that their caravans were now standing.

"It is home," they said simply. "Wherever else we go, hop-picking, potato-raising, we always come back here. Our relations are buried in the churchyard."

They then told me that they were fined daily – not only for camping but also if any of their belongings were deposited on the ground by their caravans. They showed me a summons which they had just been given for having a dustbin, two milk churns and a pram containing a live baby.

I went home and rang up the Chief Constable of the County Police, who had already helped me in a number of other problems. I said to him:

"These people appear to be law-abiding. They don't want to get into trouble. Where can they go?"

"Nowhere," he replied.

"Nowhere?" I echoed, "but that is absurd. They have been told they have to move every twenty-four hours, and if they can go nowhere it means a perpetual life of wandering. Besides they are flesh and blood, they just can't disintegrate."

"I am sorry," he said, "but that is the law as it stands. The police are as sympathetic as they can be, but you can understand we are being pressed all the time by local people who don't like gypsies to move them on. Almost as soon as a caravan stops anywhere someone will be on the telephone to the police-station demanding that they move the next day."

164

"It is absolutely ridiculous," I retorted. "If that is the law then it is time it was changed and somehow I will change it."

The following month I attended the Divisional Sessions in St. Albans. The policeman read out the charges and the Magistrates allowed me to speak.

I said that as a County Councillor I thought the gypsies ought to be rewarded, not fined, for having a dustbin.

"We keep begging people to put their litter into a dustbin, and yet when they have one we try to charge them for it. I can't imagine anything so ridiculous."

I also asked the Magistrates if they knew where the gypsies could go as they didn't want to break the law. The Magistrates looked embarrassed and mumbled that they were there only to 'administer justice'.

But that didn't stop them fining Luke Davis £3 for camping and driving a lorry on the common, although they dismissed the charge of litter.

At the next meeting of the County Council I asked if a reserve or camp could be provided for the gypsies of Hertfordshire. I told the Councillors there were a large number of true gypsies in the county and that it was essential the children who were Hertfordshire born should be given education.

I said then, and I said it again many times afterwards:

"You can't speak of democracy if there are opportunities of education for everyone *except* gypsies . . ."

A woman who was the Mayor of St. Albans rose to say that Colney Heath had suffered long enough from "those filthy litter-ridden people simply makes one's blood boil!"

I realised at that first meeting exactly the sort of opposition I was going to be up against. A lot of it was sheer mediaeval fear.

"The gypsies must go away," one Councillor screamed. "I don't care where they go, but they must go away."

A number of people called me the 'Devil's Advocate' and wrote to suggest the sooner I took the gypsies into my own garden the better; and people actually came up to

165

me in the County Hall and accused me aggressively of 'encouraging' gypsies to come into the county.

As a ruse to get some of the children to school, I put on a plea for 'common usage of the Common'. The case was taken without fee by a generous and kindly solicitor and by a clever young barrister.

We knew we were on a bad wicket because for 'common usage' one has to go back to 'time immemorial' which is 1142, and gypsies didn't come to this country until the reign of Henry VIII.

Anyway, while the case was waiting to be heard, I got nearly thirty children to school and the reports from the schoolmasters were exceptionally encouraging. One schoolmaster told me:

"We have a little girl called Mary here. She is only six but she has learned to read and write a little in six weeks. She enjoys coming to school so much that her face lights up when she attends. Everyone has remarked on it and everyone loves the child."

I asked that schoolmaster and a number of others if the gypsies came to school clean and tidy.

"They couldn't be better turned out," was the answer. "And with very few exceptions their behaviour is exemplary. To them education is a privilege."

But the villagers of Colney Heath were protesting all the time because the gypsies were camping on the common.

In 1961 just after I had to withdraw my plea of Common Usage we learned that the Rural Council intended to clear off the gypsies and dig a moat round the common so that they should not return.

The newspapers were full of stories that the gypsies were thinking of fighting, of making a last stand, to keep their traditional camping grounds, but I knew that the position was hopeless, and on August 18th, 1961 I went to Colney Heath at nine o'clock in the morning.

It was a sunny morning. There were no Members of Parliament, Councillors, Welfare Officers or clergymen. It had shocked me from the very start of the campaign

166

how little had been done by the Church to help these unfortunate people.

The only Christian contribution had been from the Vicar of Colney Heath who had turned off the water in the Churchyard because he said the gypsies were stealing it for their children.

I should have thought a cup of water was the least the Church could give towards a persecuted race of people who happened to be born gypsies.

When I arrived at Colney Heath I met Gypsy Williams by appointment and we held a short service. The gypsies stood at the doors of their caravans with tears streaming down their faces.

They sang a hymn and afterwards through a loud-speaker I asked them to go quietly telling them that nothing would be gained by fighting the police. To the Davises I added: "I will find a camp for you, that I promise."

As I said it, I had no idea of the magnitude of the task I had set myself. The caravans trundled away to no-where, the women white and silent, with a lost look, and the men tight-lipped and frightened. I watched and vowed that something should be done!

Augustus John, who was President of the Gypsy Lore Society sent me a telegram saying: "The persecution of the gypsies is based on ignorance and leads to squalor," and practically every newspaper in the country supported me in what was obviously to be a long and bitter campaign.

My telephone bell rang and an unfamiliar voice said:

"I would like to help you."

It was the Earl of Onslow who had been a Captain of the Yeoman of the Guard for nine years, and held many distinguished positions at Court.

"When I was at school at Winchester," he told me, "gypsies were constantly passing through the area on the way to the New Forest. I spent many happy hours with them and learnt more about nature-study, wild-life and folklore than in a lifetime of reading books. You will never

167

find a finer man than a genuine Romany, nor a finer friend."

We decided to form a Trust. It was called the Barbara Cartland/Onslow Trust with Lord Onslow as Treasurer.

He also brought along another enthusiast, the Earl of Birkenhead, son of the famous Lord Chancellor of Great Britain.

The first person we turned to for help was the Marquess of Salisbury. With great generosity he offered us two acres of land near Welham Green. We could have it for a pound a year, and our hopes rose at the thought of doing something so quickly.

The Davises had moved to Potters Bar where they were told if they stayed more than twenty-four hours they would be fined £5 a day. The fines in St. Albans had gone up to £4 and some of the gypsies had been moved into Bedfordshire and Cambridgeshire only to be shunted back again by the police.

They were helpless shuttlecocks in this game of slipping over the border into one county and being hurled back again. No one wanted them, they belonged nowhere!

A noisy, angry meeting of Welham Green residents made me realise that we certainly would not be allowed to put our camp on Lord Salisbury's ground.

It was frightening to arrive in stony silence and to stand on a platform being shouted and jeered at. I was so used to applause and the friendly warmth of an audience.

It was also frightening to see the violence of people's hatred. One was reminded all too clearly of the race riots that were taking place in America. Whites against blacks, whites against gypsies. What did it matter?

It was human beings against human beings, the spark which had ignited war since the beginning of time.

My friends begged me to give up the whole idea of helping the gypsies.

"You are doing yourself a lot of harm, supporting such an unpopular cause," they said.

But I knew that Ronald was inspiring and helping me.

It had become a spiritual crusade, and nothing would make me give up until I won the battle.

It is too long a story to tell in detail all that happened during the next two years. What turned the scales in my favour was that the County Council with their inevitable sense of justice – even if a little belated – came forward to support my claim, and in conjunction with the Rural District Council of Hatfield chose a site where my camp could be placed.

Unfortunately this was on ground which had been acquired by the Welwyn Garden City Development Corporation, and once again I was in direct conflict with them. They bitterly opposed the site and we had to ask for a public enquiry.

In the meantime I had written frequently to the Minister of Housing and Local Government – Sir Keith Joseph – and he was most sympathetic and promised to investigate the whole problem.

The press continued their championship, questions were raised in Parliament, and in 1963 Sir Keith Joseph announced that all local housing authorities must provide camps for their own gypsies.

It had taken three years, but I had got the law changed as I said I would.

It was a tremendous triumph, but I still lacked permission for our own camp.

Not until February 22nd, 1963 was the enquiry held in Hatfield. The Development Corporation was determined to win. They brought down both a distinguished Queen's Council and a Junior from London against myself, the Acting Clerk to the Rural Council and several officials from County Hall and the District Council.

When I was allowed to speak I said to the Inspector:

"Everyone agrees it is unjust and unfair that people should be denied education when they ask for it. But they don't want gypsies. From John O'Groats to Land's End you will find that everyone has a wonderful reason why a certain piece of land is the one place where gypsies cannot have a camp. But we must educate the children, and how can you educate people if they must move on every twenty-four hours?"

But it was the Clerk, a vivid, forceful speaker, who made the most telling remark.

"Hertfordshire gypsies are becoming a racial problem," he said. "We must remember this is Hatfield, Hertfordshire, not Little Rock, Arkansas."

The Inspector listened quietly to everything he was told. At the end of it everyone was getting a little edgy. The well-known Q.C. had a great deal to say in his summing-up for the opposition. When I asked if I could have a last word they opposed it.

"She has already spoken," the Q.C. remarked sourly.

I insisted that I had a right to speak. Rather grudgingly I was given permission.

"I only wanted to say 'thank you' to the Inspector," I said. "He has had many hours of listening to what we have had to say. I feel we all owe him a vote of thanks, whichever side we are on."

It was amazing to see the astonishment on their faces. Nobody, least of all the eminent Q.C. and his Junior from London, had thought of being grateful.

We had to wait for five months before we had the answer, but needless to say we won. It was right, it was just and I knew Ronald was by my side.

Although it had been a stern and often bitter battle, I had always known in my heart the gypsies must be allowed to get their children to school.

However, the Development Corporation had not finished with us. I was told that the enquiry had cost them something like £600 and they were smarting from the battle. When it came to making a lease for the land they said they wanted a six-foot wire fence round the camp with barbed wire on the top.

"And I suppose you want machine guns at all four corners," I said to them. "No human beings that I have anything to do with shall ever be confined by barbed wire, and I'll fight you on this if I have to take it right through Parliament."

They conceded that point but insisted on the six-foot wire fence. But when we took over the camp we found the Development Corporation had had one last word. They had removed the whole of the topsoil!

When the wire fence was erected on the barren stony ground and the concrete wash-house and basins had been put in position I felt in despair. Anything more like Belsen, with the exception that the barbed wire was missing, it was difficult to imagine.

The gypsies moved in. For over a month I did not go near them. I just felt I couldn't face that ghastly camp. It cost all the money I had raised. I had in fact written five thousand letters to get in donations of £1,500.

The churches had been extremely generous. Nearly all the Bishops, the Archbishop of York and His Eminence, the Archbishop of Westminster had contributed. So had many of my personal friends who could ill afford it and several old-age pensioners had sent me postal-orders for a shilling or half-a-crown.

After several weeks the Chief Public Health Inspector of the Hatfield Rural District Council, who had been a friend and supporter all through the controversy, rang me up.

"Have you seen your camp?" he asked.

I drew in my breath.

"Here it comes," I thought. "What has gone wrong now?"

"It is the most wonderful thing I have ever seen," he went on. "Do go and see it."

I went down and was absolutely astonished. In the short time since they had moved in, the gypsies themselves had transformed that horrible empty place into something very beautiful.

They had laid lawns round their caravans and planted seeds. They had put in shrubs and potted flowers; they had scrounged pieces of wood and made a little enclosure for each of the five caravans. They had tar-macked the path down the centre of the camp.

171

It was quite fantastic, and they kept telling me how happy they were.

"It is the first time in our lives," they said, "we have woken up in the morning without a policeman hammering on the window telling us to move on. We want our camp to have a name and we would like to call it "Barbaraville".

To-day the gypsies are all investing in small chalets. Their caravans are always kept spotless, so they are saving up to buy wooden huts where they can wash and cook and thus keep the caravan inviolate.

They have planted a mass of shrubs, bulbs and flowers of every description. They have electric light laid on which they paid for themselves, they have a telephone, and I have just added a bath to the camp.

A great number of people still hate gypsies, but many are learning to live with them. At the camp just down the road from 'Barbaraville' put up by the County Council there are thirty caravans.

Nearly fifty children have been christened in the parish Church, and in the schools they are all integrating so easily that no one realises they are gypsies.

This is the beginning. Once gypsies have got used to walls it will not be so hard to persuade them in the future to live in houses. In this small congested island, is there really room for twenty-five thousand gypsies, illiterate and unwanted, being moved from place to place?

Altogether there are forty-five thousand gypsies and followers, many of whom are didicoys or rough types who have taken to a moving life because they wish to avoid responsibility. But whatever they may be, I believe that their children must be educated.

Ronald believed that we cannot give to one and withhold from the other, and all children, of whatever creed or colour, must be given the chance of education and of becoming decent and responsible citizens of the land in which they have been born.

"Barbaraville" was an inspired crusade, it is now a dream come true.

1965

Cote d'Azur
South of France

To-day Ian, Glen and I visited Notre-Dame de Laget.

This is a lovely 16th century Church situated beyond La Turbie, over the high hills above Monte Carlo.

Few people whose eyes are fixed on the green baize tables know it exists.

Notre-Dame de Laget is the patron Saint of Accidents. All the way round the small Church itself, redolent with faith and holiness, there is an outer wall.

On these are hung hundreds of pictures painted or drawn in gratitude by those who owe their lives to Notre-Dame de Laget.

Some are very well done, some are funny in their rough construction. All are very touching in their sincerity and unshakeable belief that the artist's prayers had been heard.

I never go to the South of France without visiting Laget. To-day we all three said a prayer in the beautiful decorated Church and lit candles in front of the Saint's statue. We also bought medallions, I always carry one in my handbag.

This evening we dined in Nice and on our way back to Cap Estel where we are staying, we stopped on the Corniche Road to look at the battleships which are lit up in the harbour near Cap Ferrat.

Suddenly round the corner travelling very fast came a French car. It scraped the side of our car, buckling and damaging the body.

Had the impact been even two inches closer I would have been killed and so might one if not both of my sons.

I know it is due to Notre-Dame de Laget that we are shaken but unhurt.

1965

London

I was asked to lunch a few days ago by Lady Dowding, a dear friend who introduced 'Beauty without Cruelty' – the Cosmetics which are made without any animal ingredients in them.

Any profits from the sales are spent in alleviating cruelty to animals and Muriel Dowding has fought against the bestial clubbing to death of baby seals, the horrors in many abattoirs, the use of rabbits in experiments with hair lacquer, and a thousand other ways in which mankind exploits the animal world.

She was married to Air Chief Marshal Lord Dowding the brilliant head of Bomber Command, who was an ardent spiritualist. He produced several wonderful books, the first being *Many Mansions*, which helped thousands of those who were bereaved and without hope.

The description of how when we first die we are met by a Guide, who helps and looks after us, is very moving and very convincing.

I lunched with Muriel Dowding at her Club and when I arrived there was another woman with her who I heard say as I arrived:

"It is wrong to wear cultured pearls as the process by which they are obtained is cruel to the oyster."

As I was wearing four rows of cultured pearls at the time, I thought this rather nonsense. Muriel however, introduced us and said her friend was psychic and received great powers from the spirit world.

We sat down to lunch and since Muriel knows I am not

a vegetarian but believe that protein is essential to good health, she says:

"You order what you like Barbara, I know you prefer meat. My friend and I will have eggs."

I did as she suggested and asked for a Minute Steak. When it came it looked delicious, but as I raised a piece to my mouth it smelt and tasted so revolting that to swallow even the tiniest piece would not only be impossible but would make me physically sick.

I realised immediately that it had been cursed by Lady Dowding's friend.

I messed it about on my plate so as not to make a scene, but for the next three days any meat smelt of putrefaction and I was forced willy-nilly to be a vegetarian!!

1966

❦

Madras
India

Ian, Glen and I are staying in Madras at Raj Bhavan (The Governor's House). The Governor is the Maharajah of Mysore and we are meeting him later in his Palace.

His personal astrologer comes to make out our horoscopes with palm leaves. He speaks no English and everything he says has to be translated. So what he tells us can't be thought-reading unless our thoughts are in a universal language.

Shuffling the palm leaves he says I will live until I am eighty-five and will have no worries until I join the lotus feet of the Lord.

I am to have a 'wonderful era' in the years to come, I will acquire wealth and will travel all over the world for which I have an 'irrepressible desire'.

What interested me more in Madras was a visit yesterday to the Theosophical Society which stands in a large estate on the Adyar River.

Having read so much about Madame Blavatsky I hoped I should feel the presence of the Great Beings – the Masters – who she believed, had completed their human evolution but continued to guide and develop us. It was possible she said to get in touch with them.

There was only however, a feeling of peace and tranquillity as we stood in the shade of the largest banyan tree in India.

Three thousand people have sat there, a Universal Brotherhood of Humanity without distinction of race, creed, sex, caste or colour.

Perhaps this is what the Masters intended?

1966

Madras
India

I am deeply impressed at meeting G. Rajagopalachari, always known as Rajaji, one of the great personalities of India.

He was acting Viceroy and Governor General after Lord Mountbatten and is head of the Swatantra (or Conservative Party).

After living in great palaces, waited on by hundreds of servants, he now lives in a tiny house comprising one room and a kitchen and is looked after by one servant.

At eighty-eight he speaks clearly and forcefully and his eyes are still bright with the fire which made him one of the most formidable revolutionaries against British rule.

"It is a pity the British ever left India," he says to me.

"How can you say that?" I cry. "We imprisoned you for eight years."

He has no bitterness, no recriminations, no regrets.

I am touched by his enormous understanding, his compassion, his simple way of life and his vibrant personality.

I knew as I said goodbye I would never see him again, but I will never forget him.

1966

❧

Mysore
India

We have reached Mysore and are housed in an enormous and magnificent mansion built by the British for the President and now used by the Government for special guests.

The rooms are in the Georgian style, colossal, lofty and, as we are the only people staying here, rather eerie.

Last night as I was lying in my vast bedroom in a four-poster bed draped with mosquito netting, I was aware that I was not alone.

A British Officer in 18th century uniform was in the room. He was a middle-aged man, red in the face, very hot and cross. He threw himself down in a chair and ordered a native servant to pull off his boots.

He cursed the man for being slow and I knew he was worried by local problems and lonely in himself, as only a man can be when he is far from home.

His boots are removed as he drinks a whisky and soda and he commands the servant to fetch him a woman from the town. Even as he asks for one, I know it will not help his loneliness or assuage his longing for England and home.

1966

Bombay
India

How much animals mean in our lives! And yet so often we take them for granted. In India animals are never destroyed, not even the rodents which destroy the crops.

Yet I often wonder if the Indians really love those they preserve so carefully even when we would think it kinder to put them to sleep.

That because of their love for us they stay with us after death I have proved by my own ghost dog at Camfield, and I know one woman who will have many dogs, seen or unseen, with her in this life and I am sure the next.

We are in Bombay staying with the Governor. To-night we dined with an elegant and *chic* Parsee who has a luxury flat high up in the most expensive quarter of Malabar Hill.

When we arrived four strange-looking dogs, who were waiting outside the building, greeted us with wagging tails.

"What extraordinary breeds," I murmured to my sons as we went up in the lift.

Inside the flat we were greeted by five more dogs, all unidentifiable. Over an excellent dinner I learnt that these were all deserted or ill-treated animals which our hostess has rescued from some pitiable plight or death.

Since there was no more room inside her flat, the dogs downstairs come every evening to be washed and fed. They know they must wait until the guests leave. Then our hostess will bath them, give them a meal and let them sleep in the garage until morning.

During the day they are turned out to fend for themselves, but they always return punctually at nightfall.

I wrote a poem about one of my own beloved Pekinese who was run over. He was proud, independent and obstinate, but loyal, loving and whole-heartedly mine.

For years you walked beside me every day,
For years you slept upon my bed.
You showed your love in every way,
I can't believe that you are dead.

If there's an after-life for me,
Then I'd be lonely without you.
I must be sure that you will be
With me, whatever I may do.

So I pray to God who made you and me,
Who in death swept us apart,
To book a place in the 'Great To Be'
For a dog with a loving heart.

1966

Bombay
India

We are taken to see the part of Bombay where the prostitutes stand in the doorways of small cell-like rooms and wait for customers. Ian attempts to take a picture of them with his cine-camera, but they disappear inside.

He then tried to take the crowds but our guide says to him:

"Do not photograph Muslim women, they resent it."

"Just one shot," Ian replies.

His camera jams. There is nothing wrong with it but when the film is developed there are at that part of it long red lines like streaks of blood.

Addition: When we are at Ankar Wat in 1968 we are shown a temple where the same thing had happened the previous day.

The temple, over-grown with the trunks of trees, the branches entwined among the stones, is dark and mysterious; I feel a strong presence in it.

A woman who tried to take a photograph was told not to do so but she persisted. Her camera jammed and would not work for twenty-four hours.

1967

London

Donald Campbell, whom I knew and liked enormously, is dead and I learn that two hours before he attempted to beat his own world record he shuffled a pack of cards and drew out two – the Ace and the Queen of Spades.

"These are the same cards that Mary Queen of Scots turned over before her execution," he told a friend. "I think that someone in my family will die soon."

Donald's speedboat turned a fatal somersault at three hundred miles an hour.

I know that Donald was very superstitious. I ask myself if under the same circumstances, feeling as he must have felt, I would have been brave enough to cancel the experiment.

Most people would rather face death than ridicule, and they are afraid of trusting their instincts and their senses.

Yet how often, because we are cowards do we risk or face disaster unnecessarily?

Addition: Later Donald constantly talked to his wife in séances and she was completely convinced that he was there with her.

1967

Mexico

Ian, Glen and I were motoring from Taxco to Mexico City when by the roadside I caught a glimpse of some interesting Indian paintings for sale.

I made Ian, who was driving, turn back and I found the paintings were very colourful and attractive.

The Indians selling them were stolid with flat expressionless faces, who gave no indication whether they were pleased or not at the sale of four examples of their craft.

I brought the paintings home and had them framed. I hung three in the bathrooms at Camfield and gave one to Ian for his flat in London.

I was suddenly aware that in the happy atmosphere of my home there was something disruptive which I could feel quite vividly.

I realised that the paintings had been painted with hatred – perhaps for the white man. I was conscious of the enmity and I knew I could not keep them.

I had all four of them and their frames burnt in the garden, and after that the peace and happiness of the house remained undisturbed.

1967

Jamaica

When we arrived in Jamaica from Mexico, the first thing I did was to send Ian to swim far out into the sea to 'drown' a charm I had been given.

A round stone with coral arms and painted eyes, it was supposed to save me from the Evil Eye, but I felt it was evil in itself.

Free of this bad magic, we were told to-day that we must meet the Bird Woman.

We drove up a rough twisting road which climbed higher and higher up the verdant hills covered with palm trees, tropical foliage and flowering shrubs.

Suddenly, right on the edge of a precipice, we found a little house. Outside there was a high bird-cage, and perched on a tree, which grew close against the veranda, were hundreds and hundreds of small birds, twittering and singing as they waited for their evening meal.

Mrs. Liza Salmon had been a W.A.A.F. in the last war. She had come out to Jamaica to visit her brother who was living in Kingston and had decided not to return to England. Instead, she started a sanctuary for birds.

I sat on the terrace and tiny green and black humming-birds perched on my finger and drank sugar and water from a small bottle. They were fearless and so trusting that I felt they had never known the evils of civilisation.

How much does fear disrupt, spoil and destroy the happiness of ordinary people? Fear of poverty, of loneliness, of failure, of illness, of growing old?

1968

Ankor Wat
Cambodia

We wander in the damp heat round the fantastic temples, climb hundreds of steps, see where the jungle has entwined its branches round their roofs and tree-trunks have grown indivisibly into their walls.

It is incredibly beautiful, but somehow dead and past – until we find an enormous head exquisitely carved, the stone dark with age.

It gives me the feeling that it holds age-old secrets behind its closed eyes.

If only they would open I would, I know, find an ancient wisdom and knowledge now lost to the modern world.

> *What secrets do you hide,*
> *What wisdom lies behind*
> *The faint smile which I find*
> *Provoking?*
>
> *How can I learn to-day*
> *What you knew yesterday*
> *And find the age-old way*
> *To Love?*

1969

Taiwan

Ian, Glen and I are on a trip to Taiwan and Japan. To-day we are in the National Palace Museum of Taiwan which contains the world's richest collection of Chinese art.

Men died to save these treasures for China. They were moved secretly across the country to hide them from the Japanese invaders, buried in caves, carried in sampans.

They travelled always with a desperate fear of being discovered either by the Japanese or, later by the Chinese Communists. Finally more than 24,000 pieces reached Taiwan.

It is a triumph of human endeavour, of courageous determination.

Yet in the Temple-like museum with its glazed green tiles and air-conditioned interior, the miracle of their survival is somehow lost.

I feel ashamed that the bronze vessels made hundreds of years B.C. seem dull and uninspiring, that row upon row of handleless teacups leave me cold.

The exquisite Chinese paintings, which are permeated with a sense of wholeness depicting the growing, moving life of a flower or tree, seem imprisoned behind their glass cases.

It was said of Han Cho in 1121 that he "fathoms the uttermost secrets of heaven and earth and illuminates which is not lit by sun and moon".

This is what those who died to save these ancient pictures believed, but somehow to me the "spirit, rhythm and life-movement" has been lost too.

1969

❧

Tokyo
Japan

To-day we have had the privilege, and it is a very unusual one for a foreigner, of being taken into a Japanese house.

What interested me was the 300-year-old family Temple which is in the bedroom of our host's mother.

Exquisitely carved, it is only about 5 feet high and in front of a tiny statue there was fresh food which is placed there every day, incense sticks, two candles and a bell.

The Japanese of course believe in Ancestor worship, and the present head of the house told me that he prays at the Temple every morning and evening.

By ringing the bell he summons his father's spirit and tells him in detail what has occurred during the day.

"I report everything to my father," he says.

His voice as he speaks is deeply respectful and affectionate, and I find it very moving.

1969

❧

Kyoto
Japan

We have visited the Kiyomizu – the Clear Water Temple which was built in 758 B.C. It is fantastic in that part of it is built on enormous stilts which prevent it from sliding into the valley beneath.

I feel as if faith has held it up, because it is the only Temple in the whole of Japan which attracts members of all Buddhist sects – Indo, Shin, Zen and Tendai.

They will not enter each other's Temples, but they all visit Kiyomizu and pilgrims believe it is effective in pregnancy and childbirth.

It was the first time I had seen bushes, branches of trees and even plants tied with little pieces of paper almost as if they were in curlers.

I thought they were prayers just as the Tibetans and Nepalese have prayer-flags which they fly in the wind.

But it is explained that they are charm papers which people receive or buy in the Temples.

"If they do not bring what is required or seem unlucky," a Japanese said, "we give them back to the gods by tying them on the nearest bush or tree."

Could anything be sadder than so many unanswered prayers, so much lost faith?

1969

❦

Kyoto
Japan

To-day we visited Daisen-In. This is a Zen Buddhist Temple or Inn, built in 1509 with a famous garden.

Here I found what I had been seeking, a feeling that the symbolism of the plain rocks set on a bed of white gravel spoke to me.

I have studied Zen, so I know that the rock shaped as a tortoise represents the earth-bound nature of man, while the one like a crane, a bird which flies high in the sky, is man's better and higher self. Between them ran the river of life.

We saw a gravel river cascading down to where there was a small stone shaped like a tiger's head.

"That is the unruly nature of man," a monk explained, "swirling in the tragic experiences of life."

He showed us a barrier which divided the garden from the next.

"Here," he said, "you will observe the stream of life actually passes over the dam and continues to flow, symbolising the broadening of human understanding. The ship of stone is laden with the treasures of experience which are the joys and disappointments which come to us all."

Then beyond the entrance to the Temple there was a large garden with nothing in it but gravel, traditionally raked to look like waves.

Here the stream flows into nothingness where the rock that represented covetousness and greed has disappeared leaving only the white sands of purity.

The monk took us into the Temple and gave us the special green tea which is a sacred part of Zen Buddhism.

It looked rather like green pea soup but it tasted delicious, and where before I had been rather tired, I suddenly found I was full of energy again, with an added awareness of everything around me.

The great Zen Monasteries in Japan teach that the universe is not matter and mechanical processes but thought. Rutherford's and Einstein's investigations prove the same.

> *"It is proclaimed that Thought alone*
> *Was, Is and Shall Be,*
> *As a cloud that veils the moon so matter veils*
> *The face of Thought."*

1969

Nikko
Japan

Nikko is lovely, and to-day we drove up a twisting road with the most fantastic views, to where there is a huge lake surrounded by mountains.

"The Legends say that if you look closely you can see thousands of serpents flowing down its gentle incline," we are told. "Victims of an ancient battle between the God of one mountain and the God of another."

I couldn't see any serpents, but as we drove down a twisting and frightening road we saw the hill monkeys which are very rarely observed and are supposed to bring great good luck.

We reached the Toshogu Shrine which is the most wonderful Temple I have ever seen. It is painted every twenty years by the family who first dedicated it and consists of twenty-two buildings including a five-storey pagoda.

Here there were golden Buddhas and the original monkey carving of "See no evil, hear no evil, speak no evil."

They have carried this message all over the world and I am sure much good has come from it.

It may be the crying dragon, the phoenixes in brilliant colours, the priests in their green robes, but I find here, unlike most Temples in Japan, an atmosphere of sanctity and endeavour.

1971

Bali

In my bedroom there is a Barong Mask with its long red tongue out. He is always associated with white magic and good luck.

Last night we saw one of the strangest dances in the world. In a tiny village surrounded by the Jungle, we sit in a hall with open ends to watch the Ketcha or Monkey Dance.

One hundred and fifty men take part and the deep, strange humming of their voices, the rhythmic rise and fall of their arms as they enact a play, is hypnotic.

One feels one is moving with them and the demons and Rama King of the monkeys are all very real.

We saw Besakih, the Mother Temple of all the 10,000 Bali temples built 3,000 feet up on the Gunung Agung Volcano.

Here there is a long flight of steps flanked by stone demons wearing checked festive cloaks rising higher and higher.

There was a High Priest resplendent with a great gold crown on his head conducting a Service on a platform under a gold canopy.

I watch the women taking offerings to the Open Lotus Shrine dedicated to the Spirit of Sun. Their faith shone in their dark eyes and an aura from the sun seemed to envelope them.

1971

Bali

I asked to see a witch-doctor who is very important in the Balinese religion, but instead I was taken to the most important fortune-teller in Bali.

He was to my surprise, a thin young man sitting on a comfortable cool veranda, and I was told he had given up an important Government post to work with the spirits.

He spoke English quite well. We talked to him for some time. He didn't tell us anything of great importance except that he said to me:

"You travel all over the world seeking. So far you have only touched the branches of the tree, you have not yet reached the roots."

When he had finished, he informed us that as it was twelve o'clock he could not charge us anything, because the gods who directed him stopped their work at eleven-thirty.

It was the first time that I had ever known that they kept office hours!

1972

Rio
South America

We are visiting South America and have flown first to Rio. It is fascinating and the view from the Christus is fantastic.

To-night our guide has offered to take us to find the real Mucumba (or Voo-doo) not the sort which is put on for the tourists.

We drive through the hills thickly covered in trees for a long way. The guide tells us that the Mucumba are frightened of the police and keep their meetings very secret.

Suddenly by the side of the road we see a small figure of a goddess, obviously left behind in a hurry.

A little further on we come to a place where the meeting has been held. There are two or three dozen plates holding a variety of offerings to the gods. There is a strong smell of cheap brandy and cigars.

The car stops and as I wait to get out I have a strange and terrible feeling of evil. It is so overwhelming I beg my sons to drive away at once.

There is no movement in the darkness of the trees except for a dog who is running round eating the offerings for the gods.

Yet I feel there are eyes watching me. The menacing pressure of either the living or the dead.

I hurry everyone away. I was afraid, really, horribly afraid.

1972

Salvador
South America

To-day we visited the most beautiful church in the world – the Sao Francisco. Every inch of its carving is covered in gold and it glows with a thousand different lights.

From there we see the platform where thousands of slaves chained together were sold, and go on to lunch in the Solar Du Unhao which was built in the 17th Century.

The Restaurant is underground in what were the slave-quarters of a large sugar-mill. It has rooms, I learn, in which the slaves were tortured.

The slaves themselves used it as a meeting-place during the Taylors' Conspiracy through which they hoped to win their liberty.

I try not to remember the horrors which had been perpetrated within those thick stone walls, but I keep thinking of the insatiable cruelty of man to man.

Actually I am sure one should not go to such places. Who knows what impression it kindles in the mind to emerge later in strange unaccountable actions.

For the same reason violence on the television is dangerous. One may say 'it is all make-believe', but the brain retains everything it sees and hears.

How many young minds are we positively inoculating with a taste for crime, brutality and even for sexual perversions.

1973

Tunisia
North Africa

Glen and I are in Tunisia, we have motored nearly a thousand miles visiting the Roman ruins.

In Dougga, which was beautiful with spring flowers growing round the ruins, I was suddenly vividly aware of the unhappiness of the women who followed in the train of the all conquering Roman Armies.

I could almost hear their tears and their complaining voices. I would feel their unhappiness at being torn away from their homes, their friends, and all that was familiar.

They had to live in a new hostile land with the unceasing agony of wondering if their men might be killed or injured.

I wrote this poem to –

"THE SOLDIER'S WIFE"

Did you suffer in an alien land?
Did you weep at being far from Rome?
Did the conqueror's foot on miles of sand
Mean anything except it was not home?

The Romans won and lost the world,
The Greeks, the Goths, the French all fought
For power, while holy Spain unfurled
Horrors and cruelty of another sort.

So many broken lives, so many tears,
What does it mean in centuries to come?
Can ruins tell us of the fears
That women feel, while men still beat the drum.

1974

Khajuraho
India

Back in India, to-day Glen and I visited the Khajuraho Temples, which were built between A.D. 900 and 1100 under the great Chandela Kings and were only discovered accidentally by an Englishman who was out shooting.

When the jungle which had covered them had been removed, the most perfect and magnificent sculptures were revealed, which show these Temples as masterpieces of the art and architecture of the Rajput age.

Where the Temples have been cleaned, the statues really look as if they had been carved yesterday because, owing to the climate, the majority of them are in a perfect state of preservation.

Some of the beautiful and ecstatic statues are undeniably erotic, which is, of course, part of the Hindu Religion. Life in all its physical aspects is worshipped, and ecstasy and passion are part of the Divine.

The Temples stand in a beautiful garden with huge flowering shrubs and some very fine trees. It is difficult to describe the marvellous atmosphere which pervades the whole place and how the beauty of the Temples uplifts the mind.

After seeing the Temples I was taken to see a Saddhu, a Holy Man, who lived just outside the village.

Unfortunately, unlike other Saddhus I had met, he could not speak English, but I asked him what he thought of the future, and our Guide translated his reply:

"Only by love will there ever be any understanding between nation and nation and man and man."

1975

Sri Lanka

The Earl Mountbatten of Burma has always told me one place I should visit because it was so beautiful was Sri Lanka – which we called Ceylon when I was at school.

Glen and I therefore decided to go there this Spring. We were fascinated by Colombo, by the exquisite loveliness of Kandy and the tea country above it.

A very strange thing happened to me when I was there. Before I left London I was entertained at the Ceylon Tea Centre in Regent Street by Mr. Samaraskara of the Ceylon Embassy and the Venerable Dr. Saddhatissa who is head of the Buddhist Movement in England.

As we were in the hall leaving the building I said to the Doctor:

"Thank you for all your good wishes. I hope that you will pray for us while we are away."

Immediately he closed his eyes and started to pray which rather surprised the people who were coming in to buy packets of tea!

However, when translated it was a very charming prayer for our safety and happiness and I felt his blessings would ensure us a happy time.

Up in the hill above Kandy we stayed in the Hunas Falls Hotel. It is built by a cascade and looks over the lovely valley of the tea country. I went to bed early after a long day, then suddenly outlined on a wall in the darkness I saw very clearly the Venerable Dr. Saddhatissa.

What was interesting was that just as I had seen the Cardinal in Vienna, he was high above my head but I could see him absolutely clearly for several minutes.

I knew then that he was still praying for us and when I returned home I asked if that was so. He agreed he had been thinking about us a great deal.

1975

Manilla
The Philippines

Glen and I have come here from Sri Lanka. I am very anxious to consult the faith-healers who have been written about in the newspapers at home as achieving miraculous cures.

I want their help as I am suffering great pain.

Glen and I had visited Agra during a visit to India and found there was a full moon that night. We decided of course to see the Taj Mahal by moonlight.

There is a very high step at the entrance and I caught my toe on it and fell forwards. I cut my leg but thought nothing about it at the time.

We sat looking at the incredible exquisite beauty of the tomb built by love which glowed like a pink pearl against the star-studded darkness.

When I returned to England I found the base of my spine had been displaced. The only suggestion from the doctors was an operation which is usually only 50% successful.

This was on top of severe back trouble I had been experiencing for some time which made it ache especially at night.

This evening when we arrive in Manilla I find one of the people to whom I have been given an introduction is attending a party in the restaurant at the top of the hotel.

We met our friend who is sitting at a table with three Ambassadors. After we have talked about our trip I tell them I am anxious to meet a genuine faith-healer.

"That's easy," our host exclaims. "The best one, who treats me, is here to-night."

I am surprised when he points out a small good-looking young man, very well dressed and dancing energetically. I arrange to see him the following day.

We drive for miles in the Suburbs until we find a rough wooden hut. It contains pews in which two or three people are sitting, waiting to be seen by the Healer.

Glen and I occupy a pew. After a little while the Healer comes from another room, greets me and says:

"I'll see you next but I must have my coffee and a cigarette first!"

Five minutes later I am taken into a tiny cell, it is nothing else. A woman undoes the back of my dress and I lie face downwards on a bed.

The Healer prays and works in silence touching my back where it has been aching.

"The power of God will heal you," he says confidently.

He charges no fee but one is invited to put a donation in a box.

I have now had three treatments and leave tomorrow.

I want to say I am better but it would not be true.

Addition: Some months later the newspapers were full of stories of spirit surgery which was proved to be bogus and a confidence trick performed with rabbits blood.

Everyone in Manilla was talking of the spirit surgeons. I was assured by those who knew the country that they did exist in the hills, but would not parade their gifts and were not to be found in the towns.

201

1975

Camfield Place
Hatfield

I have achieved the world record by writing twenty books in a year. Nineteen novels and a Cookery book.

It is extraordinary, but I am writing with less effort and more than I wrote when I was twenty-five.

A great deal of the energy I have is due to ginseng and the amazing root which has such magical qualities that for centuries the Chinese, believing it was the source of eternal youth, kept it only for their Emperors.

To-day it is available for everyone, but I also have spiritual help with my books.

When I want a plot for a new novel I tell my sub-conscious. I do this deliberately and with care, because if I am not careful I have several plots thrusting themselves on my brain at the same time.

Usually some small thing triggers off the plot and it is there! It may be a patch of vivid colour, the sound of music, a sentence in a book, something quite trivial, but the whole story falls into place and all I have to do is the research.

This I enjoy and I read about twenty to thirty books for the background of each novel. When this is done it is just a question of getting down the words.

I dictate my novels and it is almost as if I am told what to say. This is not to suggest I am in a trance, it is only as if I listen for the right word and it is part of the rhythm of a sentence.

My heroes and heroines live with me, and just as I see the house, the view or a place I am describing quite clearly in my mind's eye – so I see my people.

Sometimes they are so real I wonder if like Madame Alexandra David-Neel I have actually produced them! Supposing after I have finished they still exist as I first created them, just as every word we say continues as part of creation for all time.

Or have they lived before and I have picked up their vibrations and recreated them? Or may I have known them in a previous incarnation?

This is a fascinating thought and I wrote a poem to express that last idea.

"TO A PORTRAIT OF A GEORGIAN GENTLEMAN"

I could feel you as I walked into the hall,
And then I saw your portrait on the wall,
And knew you were the man I'd sought
Through centuries of thought
And in my dreams.

The high cravat, the windswept curls,
The fashions of the Prince of Wales.
Bucks, Corinthians, the 'Beau Ton' set,
You were one of them, and yet,
You too had dreams.

A rake – but with a twinkling eye,
A gamester, yet I wonder why.
While you were bored and cynical,
Women found you irresistible
But elusive.

Was it because you looked for me?
From other centuries past when we
Had loved each other passionately,
And known that no-one else could be
The same?

I search for you, I always will,
But you are dead – while I am still
Alive – yet in each 'life' where we're apart,
I'll love you in my secret heart
Until we meet again.

1976

❧

Camfield Place
Hatfield

At the beginning of 1976 it was two years since I had fallen down in the Taj Mahal and put the base of my spine out of place.

I had seen six osteopaths, had acupuncture, injections and traction which was invented by the Catholics for the infidels!

Nothing had been any use and I was getting really desperate. I sent out in the life-force a cry for help and I also, as I have done often before in an emergency, prayed to St. Jude.

I am not a Catholic like my mother, but I do believe that faith from centuries of praying accumulates like a great power-house and we can draw upon it.

St. Jude is the patron saint of Lost Causes and he has never failed me in a real emergency.

The next day a friend telephones and says she has seen a programme on television in which Ludovic Kennedy interviewed a man who was wonderful with backs.

By this time I was in agony day and night. I wrote to the B.B.C. for the man's name and was put in touch with a Major Bruce MacMannaway. I had no idea when I kept an appointment with him that he was a healer.

He sat me on a stool in front of him, and without my having to undress very gently put my spine into place. Then he said: "Now we will put on the heat".

I thought he was using a machine but after I had felt waves of heat rippling up and down my spine, I found it came just from his hands.

After one treatment I had no pain in my back and

205

could get out of bed quite quickly and easily, but I was left with very bad arthritis.

This was to be expected as the spine had been out of place for eighteen months. I could hardly walk or turn over in bed.

Again I prayed for help and I was guided quite clearly to take Adele Davies's book *Let's Get Well* from my bookshelf. I found that she recommended Calcium Pantothenate as a cure for arthritis.

With all my experience of natural health I had never heard of it, but I discovered with some difficulty that quite a lot of research had been done in this field.

To cut a long story short, with injections and tablets of Calcium Pantothenate, and of course my wonderful healer, I was cured – completely cured.

It really was a miracle!

1976

Martinique
In the Caribbean

Glen and I have arrived in Martinique. A fascinating island, with its rain forests, its hedges of crimson hibiscus flowers, its French food.

We are staying at Lez Ritz. Originally a planter's house, it has been converted into a hotel, the slaves quarters are chalets, the great store-houses a dining-room.

We are in what was the planter's house. When we arrive we find in the Salon with its glassless windows an exhibition of dolls, ranging from Elizabeth I to Josephine Baker.

To my surprise they are all made from leaves, the beautiful exotic leaves of the trees in the forests.

At night the darkness is full of mystery and as I lie in a huge four-poster bed I think I hear in the silence the Voodoo drums of the slaves.

A story is there in my mind and the characters in it are in the house: I feel them, see them clearly, hear their voices and know they are concerned with dark magic and the dolls.

1976

Athens
Greece

Yesterday Glen and I motored from Athens to Delphi. I had longed to see where the Temple of Apollo had stood and where the Sacred Oracle had attracted pilgrims in their thousands.

It was a sunny day and the light which is so essentially Greece was very beautiful and transformed everything. I prayed as we travelled towards Delphi in the words of Ajax to Zeus:

> *"Make the sky clear and grant us to see with our eyes; In the light be it."*

We reached Delphi and I climbed to where a level platform with a few huge columns is all that remains of the Temple of Apollo. The white stone gleamed in the sunshine, and while Glen went on up to the Stadium I sat beneath the Shining Cliffs – the Phaedriades – which scintillated in the sun with myriad points of multi-coloured reflected light.

I looked up at them and had the feeling that the valley, the mountains and the sea were slowly revolving in front of them.

I hoped to have an experience in the Sanctuary of Delphi itself but instead I had a glimpse of the loveliest view in Greece and for a second stepped through the Looking-Glass.

I can't explain in words what happened there and what has happened before. But suddenly the blue sea in the little port in the Gulf of Krisa where the pilgrims landed, the valley of grey-blue olive trees, the blue mountains curving away to left and right, were crystallised with light.

The view leapt into my mind and into my heart as Apollo had leapt from a ship disguised as a star to climb the steep road to the lair of the dragon who guarded the Shining Cliffs and slay him.

He then announced to all the gods that he claimed possession of all the territory he could see from where he was standing.

He was, among other things, the god of good taste and he chose the loveliest view in Greece.

It was mine in that fleeting second of time, and I not only saw the strange glitter and shining of the light but heard the mysterious quivering, the beating of silver wings with which Apollo passes through the darkness.

Then there was only a beautiful view and the scattered ruins. In A.D. 362 the Oracle speaking for the last time had said:

> *No shelter has Apollo, nor sacred*
> *laurel leaves;*
> *The fountains now are silent;*
> *the voice is stilled.*

But as Glen returned to me and we climbed down to the Sanctuary of Athene, the plot for a new book was there, waiting only for me to dictate it. I even knew the title – 'Kiss the Moonlight'.

1977

❦

La Paz
Bolivia

Glen and I are in La Paz – 12,400 feet up, at the highest city in the world. A mountain covered in snow towering over the fertile valley is breath-takingly beautiful, but we want to see the witch-doctors' market.

A narrow cobbled street rises sharply from a square. On one side of it are the Indian Amazon women who are skilful in warfare and very shrewd in business.

All wearing brown bowler hats, beautiful coloured shawls and very full skirts, they are selling herbs, charms and, most important, the dead embryos of lamas.

These are buried at the four corners of any new house with a bag of coloured sweets to placate the Goddess of the soil.

They will not be photographed as they believe the camera takes their souls from them and that moreover they will suffer excruciating pain when they die.

An Indian woman gives me three small white charms – a hand to denote money; a fist for power and strength; a couple linked together for passionate love.

1977

Lake Titicaca
Bolivia

To reach the highest lake in the world (two and a half miles high) we leave La Paz at six o'clock in the morning and drive over incredibly rough, dusty roads for two hours.

The lake is rough and I hope I won't be sick as the waves splash against the hydrofoil.

We stop at the Sacred Island of the Sun from where the first Inca King and his Queen Mama Occio travelled to Cuzco to establish an Empire which lasted for five centuries. I drink a drop of the water from the spring of Eternal Life.

When God made South America I am told he gave every country some great asset – gold, minerals, fertile soil, etc. But he forgot Bolivia.

"What are you going to do about us?" the Bolivians asked indignantly.

"You can have everything that is left," God replied.

So they have gold, tin, copper, silver, tungsten, lead, zinc, tropical fruits, alpacca, vicuna, chinchilla and a thousand other valuable commodities.

"Unfortunately," I am told solemnly, "God forgot to give to us lazy Bolivians the will to utilise them."

1977

❦

Cuzco
Peru

Here in the ancient capital of the Incas, a little breathless from the height, I see the face of the many-rayed Sun God in the elaborate gold-covered carvings of the amazingly beautiful Catholic churches.

To attract the Indians to the 'true Faith' the priests also incorporated mirrors in the carving, because those who looked in them thought they saw the reflection of their souls.

As in the churches in Mexico, the cruelty inflicted by the Spaniards on a conquered people has left an atmosphere of agonised faith and suffering.

What enchants me all over Peru are the lovely 16th century pictures painted by natives under direction from the priests. But they are all peeling, bulging, rotting and no-one seems to care!

Obsessed by the Inca stones which have lasted for over five thousand years and will last another five, and by the gold carvings in the churches, they have neglected the pictures.

To me, the faces of the saints are full of the spiritual suffering endured by the artists, and the cry of their souls for compassion and help has been transmitted to canvas.

I know that a message of deep significance and inspiration is being lost to the world as these pictures in the moist climate are crumbling into dust.

1977

Machu Picchu
Peru

I am sitting looking at the Sacred stones on which the Incas worshipped the Sun. This once great city was built on the top ridge of cliffs which rise 2,000 feet above the rapids of the Urnbamba river.

The mountains all round it rise almost perpendicularly and are so overwhelmingly majestic, so fantastically unusual that I feel, as the Incas felt, I am in the presence of the Gods.

Machu Picchu was the final refuge for the Inca Virgins of the Sun from the treacherous cruelty of the Spanish Conquerors. A sun-dial, carved from a massive rock, was used by Inca Astronomers to make solstices and equinoxes.

Built of white granite, the existence of this Sacred City was kept secret for three hundred years.

On ceremonial occasions the *Mama-Cuna* or Mother Superior of the Virgins ignited a tuft of cotton by concentrating the sun's rays with a concave bronze mirror.

When she died she was given a very beautiful resting-place under a great rock and beneath a ceremonial terrace, with a superb view of the City, the wonderful canyon and snowcapped peaks.

Excavators who discovered her bones also found her small personal belongings beside her – her pottery, two large bronze shawl-pins, bronze tweezers, two sewing-needles made from plant spines, two rings, a cooking-pot and the skeleton of her dog.

The towering mountains, the frightening drop to the dangerous river, the sense of loss of an amazing civilization, the holiness of the *Mama Cuna*, all seemed to merge into a very human love for a little collie-like dog.

213

1977

Quito
Ecuador

In Peru I was interested in Simon Bolivar, but here in Quito he dominates me.

This brilliant, amazing, fascinating man who swept the conquering Spaniards out of South America after 300 years seems to be beside me.

I feel his soaring imagination, his unparalleled skill in organisation, his fantastic strategy in planning campaigns, his knowledge of men – and of women.

Bolivar's protean mind grasped everything: he arranged battles, diplomacy, education, laws, constitutions, medals and uniforms.

I find I see Quito not so much as it is, but rather as it appeared to Simon Bolivar the demi-god after the battle in 1822.

I see his face showing suffering and thought, his supple body moving gracefully with every prancing step of his magnificent white horse.

He is beside me, he is real, he vibrates on the thin air!

I feel his exhaustless energy galvanising his three exhausted secretaries, ideas pouring from him, letters directed to every part of South America, his plan for the Gran Colombia, his ceaseless, feverish desire for women!

In the day time I think of him in the cool rooms of the Residential Palace creating a new order for Ecuador.

At night I hear the soft foot-step of his mistress Manuela Saenz, as covered by a dark cloak, guided by a hurricane-lamp and escorted by two huge dogs, she answers his simple message –

"Come to me . . . Come . . . Come now."

Then there is only the distant call of the night watch:
"Ave Maria, a June night. All is well."

He haunts me, this great man who started life as a
Marquis and a millionaire and ended it in exile, without
a peso to his name.

To-day as the Saviour of South America he is enshrined in the hearts of the people to whom he brought
freedom and in mine.

There can be no dividing of ourselves,
You are of me, as I am part of you.
And if our earthly paths uncrossed
Have left us unreflected, incomplete
In this brief life, what matter,
When the future and the past are ever ours.

1977

Camfield Place
Hatfield

I have recently written a novel called *Look, Listen and Love* and I think those words are a good guide for those who seek the World Behind the World.

In this book I have only written of what to me have been great events, important happenings, but there have been so many others.

Glancing back places stand out with a clarity which has imprinted them on my mind:

A small wayside shrine in Jaipur when we stopped to look at the Amber Fort; the leafless trees against a winter sky at home; a broken Roman pillar in Tunisia; a shimmer of moonlight on the lake surrounding the Palace on Udapur.

When I have looked at these I have felt rising within me a spiritual thrill more intense, more insistent than anything physical and yet as vividly real and always unforgettable.

We pray, we meditate, we concentrate, whatever you like to call our efforts to reach the Divine, but we must also listen for an answer. Invariably there is one, although not always immediately.

Lastly those who seek the truth know that love, which has been distorted, degraded and misunderstood, is in reality, life itself.

When we give out love we become one with the whole living breathing force of the universe and God.

A PRAYER

One thing I know, life can never die,
Translucent, splendid, flaming like the sun.
Only our bodies wither and deny
The life force when our strength is done.

Let me transmit this wonderful fire,
Even a little through my heart and mind,
Bringing the perfect love we all desire
To those who seek, yet blindly cannot find.